Faye Whitefield Carlton

ISLAND

HUMMINGBIRD

Growing up in the Bay Islands of Honduras

Utila, Roatan, Barbarat

To order additional copies of this book, contact:

fayewhitefieldcarlton@gmail.com or amazon.com

THIS BOOK IS DEDICATED

IN LOVING MEMORY

OF MY SISTER

SADIE JACKSON

Although the world keeps turning and the sun comes up each day life for me has never been the same since you were called away to heaven. You were such a special kind, quiet, and good person and have left the sweetest memories and thoughts behind. I only wish there was a way that I could see you again to thank you for the joy you brought into this life of mine...I will forever love and miss you my sister, my mother, my friend.

Faye Whitefield, standing in front of the lagoon, behind her grandmother's home.

Section 1

ISLAND DAYDREAMS OF ENCHANTED SPELLS

Barefoot and exploding with island energy, the seven-year-old girl was running wide-open with her red curls bouncing and popping in the warm-blowing tropical breeze and her yellow cotton dress flowing behind her, never once giving thought to the sharp, rocky terrain poking at her tiny feet, as she was headed in the direction of the tall coconut palms on the white sandy beachside of the crystal-clear aquamarine Caribbean sea of her tiny Bay Island home of Utila. Here she would once again give way to a world of imaginary childhood daydreams; daydreams and thoughts that were as much a part of her young self as the very breath that she breathed.

Faye Whitefield, looking down upon her pretty yellow dress now wet with perspiration, flopped down under the shade of the coconut palms, waiting to catch her breath. With hands cupping her face and elbows buried deep in the soft beach sand, the little barefoot girl stared mesmerized out across the sea of endlessness, watching as wave after wave furiously came rolling in desperate need of finding home on the beach, only to be crashed against the sharp-pointed black steel rocks of the iron shore, leaving nothing behind but their white foamy presence. Straining her young eyes, she searched the horizon, trying to see the outlined mountains of the mainland just eighteen miles in the distance. And staring still further, she turned her head to the left hoping to also see the outlines of the neighboring islands of Roatan and Guanaja.

The girl was so consumed in her thoughts as her young imaginative mind rehearsed scene after scene of stories told of days long ago when Indians and pirates roamed this very beach on the place that she called home. Transfixed by her daydreams and calmly relaxed by the soothing lullaby of the ocean's waves as they slapped against the iron shore, the girl shifted around in the sand as her drooping eyes became heavy from imaginary scenes of pirate ships laden with treasure and pirates, making their way to shore in strange-looking canoes as they left lines in the sand, dragging heavy chests of gold and jewels. This was more than her jaded eyes could take. Her head of reddish curls drooped softly to the sand as her eyes were enveloped in a peaceful sleep.

Awakened two hours later by chirping sounds of birds in nearby trees, little Faye bolted upright with a new scene in her mind: her mother letting her 'have it' for running off again. Brushing herself clean from all traces of beach sand, she determined that it was a good idea to head home.

 But not before she made a quick climb up the trunk of a coconut tree for her favorite treat of the tender flesh and sweet water of the green coconut. High up in the tree with her tiny legs and one arm wrapped tight around its trunk, with her free hand she reached up and grabbed one of the green coconuts, twisting it around and around until it broke loose from its cluster and landed in the soft sand. With the ease with which she was accustomed, she began her descent of a fast downward slide. Following the narrow path along the ocean side with the coconut swinging from her hand, she started the somewhat lengthy walk back towards home.

As the narrow and bushy path gave way to more openness, she was distracted by the scurrying sounds of iguanas as they made cracking sounds among the leaves scattered upon the ground. Stooping to pick up a handful of small rocks, the little girl's face lit up with joy, as the chase was about to begin. At a galloping speed, breathless and excited and with rocks flying in all directions, little Faye's game of iguana chasing was underway. With the iguanas desperate to find safety from their hunter, some found hiding places under rotten tree trunks lying on the ground or behind large rocks, while others dashed up to the trees, hiding among their green and brown leaves. The little girl finding their hiding places and kicking up a noise with her feet caused the iguanas to leave their places of safety as she continued to chase after her scurrying friends. Spotting a narrow tail wedged between a large rock, she dropped to one knee and, grabbing a small stick, poked through the rock's crevice at the fearful iguana. Exhausted, thirsty, and red-faced, she got to her feet, having had her fill of the iguana chasing game.

Walking now at a faster pace after seeing pictures in her mind of her mother, the little girl hurried on, kicking small rocks with her bare feet as she walked. At times coming to a slower pace, she would look around as her young mind drifted away to her island's hypnotic spells of enchantment as it spewed island beauty all around her.

The tender young mind of the little girl was captivated by scenes such as she had seen in picture books of places bustling with people and of speeding cars running through streets that were empty of children playing games, where the blue ocean sides of beaches were hidden by tall buildings. Scenes which caused such wonderment within the girl gave way to saddened thoughts that those same scenes could one day come to her small island paradise. Those changes could cause the very path that she was walking on - one where almond trees lined its sides and spilled nuts by the hundreds as they fell from their homes in the branches of the large shady trees - to one day all be gone. Little Faye felt sorrowful grief as a child would feel when her place of play could be wiped away by the blades of huge, yellow, monstrous machines as they tore away everything in their path, leaving nothing behind but open emptiness.

Coming to an even slower pace and looking up as she walked, the little girl came to a complete stop. Spying a yellow, ripe, fat almond that was hidden deep within the green foliage of the tree, her saddened thoughts quickly turned to excitement as she hurriedly made her ascent up the trunk of the almond tree. Carefully jumping from limb to limb, being mindful that her dress would not be caught and ripped by a small, pointed branch, she made her way toward the almond's hiding place. She stretched her small body out while holding onto a limb with one hand, and with the other she reached until her tiny hand made contact with the sweet, soft flesh of her prize. Finding just the right limb, she stretched her small body out, placing one arm under her head as her teeth sank into the tender flesh of the sweet almond. From her special limb in the tree, she could see and hear the roaring of the blue ocean below and the clapping sound of the wind as it made contact with the tree's leaves.

Little Faye loved her island home more than anything else in her young world, for there was hardly a place that didn't carry the footprints of her tiny bare feet.

Gazing through the leaves at the open blue sky and watching the approach of a small red bird as its tiny feet found a nearby limb, once again her mind was captured by thoughts of the picture books. Saddened still and wiping clean her small, juice-covered hands, she scurried down from the tree. With the iron shore and its scenes now far behind her and home yet a distance away, she pulled herself back from the unpleasantness of thoughts crowding her mind.

As she rounded a bend in the path that led to home, her young eyes were joyful to see in the short distance her favorite fishing place, where she spent hours sitting in her small wooden canoe anchored close to the lighthouse.

With the need for home in her mind and seeing the small wooden bridge that she had to cross just up ahead, the little girl hurried on.

Pausing halfway across the bridge and looking out to the blue ocean, she stared at the approaching motor dory with its day's catch of fish lying in its bottom as her father steered the *Miss Faye* between the bridge's posts to the lagoon that would take it home. Watching the white foamy peaks left behind by *Miss Faye*, her wandering mind was again reminiscing of conversations that she would hear as she sat in her almond tree of the fishermen as they gathered together to sit on the huge roots of the large tree in her yard, having no idea that little listening ears were above as they talked amongst themselves. The conversations they had as they talked about the island and the ways of its people were stuck in the mind of the little girl, forming pictures as she listened. As she gazed through the sun's glare, she rehearsed them in her mind over and over again as she stood upon the small wooden bridge. Remembering the stories told of her island home of Utila, sitting snugly in the warm Caribbean sea and perched on the largest barrier reef in the Western Hemisphere, brought a joyous smile to her face and caused a hypnotic spell to overtake her young mind as the scenes of her island unfolded before her eyes .

The island possessed a huge reef filled with many species of sea life that called it home. Such species were willing to share their homes with divers from around the world who would relish in the reef's natural, unspoiled beauty. The island is known for casting blue waves of crystal spells upon visitors seeking its ocean's warmth; spells so powerful with its tranquil beauty that many newcomers would settle and call it home as they lazed in hammocks sandwiched between coconut palms. With the island measuring about 13 kilometers long and just over 4 kilometers at its widest, one would call it small. But the peaceful tranquility that it produced from its smallness made for an easy, laid-back, and quiet lifestyle that was sought after by many. The coconut palms that lined its white sandy beaches stood tall and proud in their natural habitat were home to wild parrots, pigeons, and iguanas. Chanting spells of long-ago Indians might still be heard as heavy ocean winds swiftly blow through caves of freshwater hidden deep within rocky walls, revealing secrets of long-ago hidden treasure. As one was approaching the island, tiny houses could be seen along the harbor's front, nestled among the tropical foliage of the coconut and almond trees, where a small lighthouse proudly stood in the island's channel, displaying its blinking light to oncoming vessels and steering them clear from the dangers of the reef. As small passenger boats would make their approach to the island's harbor, one couldn't help but admire the beautiful green-and-white historic Methodist church as it sat on the ocean's edge, displaying its white, pointed steeple proudly towards the open sky. The sandy streets could be seen busy with people walking or riding bicycles as they went about their daily routines of making preparations for the next meal, and where children played games in the streets, for the streets were barren of vehicles. The island had just a couple of vehicles that were used primarily for transporting cargo from small boats that would arrive from the mainland bringing goods to the owners of the few small general stores. The vehicles, such as one belonging to Mr. Foster Cooper - better known as Fotee - were rarely seen at night, assuring the children's safety as they played games in the streets.

The grocery shopping custom of the islanders was a strange one. It consisted of shopping on a daily basis of three times per day or from meal to meal. To the island family, such little ones as Faye were handily used to run back and forth to the stores for any forgotten and quickly needed items. Staring at the large candy jar showing off its colorful pieces, the little girl would count any leftover pennies, hoping to buy a piece of the sweet and colorful hard candy. If one were a customer purchasing goods for a meal, the other customers always knew what that family's meal would be, as would others who were not present. Such were the interesting habits of the islanders, but as in all cultures, forces of habit are not easily broken - especially if one is content with such habits. Such were the customs that best suited everyone, as was so from the time of their ancestors. A dime's worth of flour, a nickel of sugar, a five-cent piece of butter, and so on was the normal way of life to the people of Utila.

Purchased goods were wrapped in paper or served in small brown paper bags, which, for a few pennies, the shop owner would purchase back from the customer. Many days would find the little girl rummaging through her mother's and grandmother's kitchens in search of such bags that could buy a piece of candy. But she was always met with the great temptation to blow her breath into the small bag, twist it closed, and give it a hard slap to hear the loud bang.

Hearing the squeaking sound of an approaching bicycle, the little girl was pulled back from scenes of her island thoughts.

With the need to hurry home and plans to continue the pictured memories in her mind, she crossed the bridge just in time to hear squealing cheers of laughter ringing out from swimming buddies as they jumped and played in the salty ocean water. Temporarily forgetting about her mother's scolding, little Faye quickly ran toward the sounds of cheering friends. In a hurried run down the length of the dock behind her aunt Trudy's house, with her yellow cotton dress blowing in the ocean's breeze, she made a fast jumping splash into the blue water, sending salty sprays in all directions as they made contact with cheering friends where games of diving and holding breaths were underway. The little girl dove and kicked as though she were a fish swimming deep under the salty water. Climbing up the dock's ladder with her wet dress sticking to her small frame, the little barefoot, wet, and salty Faye waved goodbyes as she ran, shivering with cold, down the dock's length.

With home now in sight and her mother again on her frightened mind, she skipped the rest of the way to the home she shared with her mother and father, two sisters, and brother.

Faye (bottom right) with her siblings Sadie, Muriel, & Gilbert.

Her home was a quaint and cozy wooden structure built on posts five feet off the ground, making a perfect place of shade for a playhouse underneath. It included a front porch that ran the full length of the house, which sat near the street, displaying a family swing hanging and held by chains which squeaked when pushed to its limit by the little curly-haired and barefoot Faye. The home's furnishings were simple and basic without added frills.

Life for the little girl was a happy one, as she lived a life of freedom running here and there as she sought her island's adventures of fun-filled places.

Note: The uniqueness of one's family should not be based upon wealth, for when wealth is depleted, the family remains.

Section 2

THE GIRL AND HER ISLAND

Little Faye, joyous that her mother didn't let her 'have it,' had something else on her mind. Quickly swallowing her supper, she ran in search of friends already playing games. The little girl hurriedly joined in and was soon lost in her favorite hiding places of hide-and-seek.

Tired now and weary from the day's events of daydreaming, chasing iguanas, and swimming, little Faye made her way back home to find such sleep that would bring with it a new dawn of tomorrow, which would bring the usual simple life for the little girl, but one in which necessary everyday tasks were not always easy.

Upon awaking, with school on her mind, she downed a fast breakfast of a slice of coconut bread and a cup of coffee.

Walking to school each morning and then back again in the afternoon with the sun beating hot upon her head of red curls, little Faye loved her class time of learning, and more so the recess with playing friends as they exchanged pickled papaya and roasted peanuts.

With recess over, the teacher passed a sheet of paper to the students and told them to describe their family life as best they could for an extra credit. Pulling her pencil that was lodged behind her ear, the little girl propped her arms on the small desk as she wondered about the new assignment. With the pencil making contact with the piece of paper, she began the task at hand.

my famly liyfe on Utila.

my famly is norml and they dont hav no xtra mony to spen.

my fater maks the mony by byldn huses for peple dat pay him mony .

and my motha stys hom cokin and stuf.

my big sista wrks at mr edwin shop but she only sits on a stol and dats all

my oda sista and motha dont wrk cose thers nothng for dem to do.

i do plnty of stupd chors

so the husbun and fater hav to do the workng to buy us fod and clos but no mor.

somtym my fater and my brodha caces fysh and sels it to rich peple.

and somtym my fater sells watamelns too.

but i also work hard cose wen my unklys Jake and Hal caches plynty of fysh den dey synd me all ova Utila to sell it to the rich peple cose they hav plynty mony and dey dont ned all of it so dey by my fysh and den i get hapy.

*dat stynkng fysh gets hevy in my hands so i get a
pyce of strng and den i tie it on a long naro rock
and den i push the rock and strng truh the stnky
fyshes moyts until it pops out the oder syde and den
i rap the strng rond my hand and den the hevy
stynky fysh is esyr to kary.*

*afta i wakl all day with the hot sun hitn me on the
hed and makyn me get da swyts and wen all the
rich peple bugt all the fysh den my unklys pys me
ten cens for selyn al the fysh and den am rich.*

*fynsh---dis papr blong to Faye Whitefield the one
wid the red hiar and freckyls.*

Raising her hand to indicate that she was finished with her
assignment, her teacher motioned her to bring it forward. Adding
it to the stack and without looking at it, the teacher told her that
she would grade it later.

With school over and some chores already done, little Faye took
off again with her fishing line and bait from her uncle's salted fish
that was hanging across the line to dry.

As she sat on the small dock behind Mrs. Caroline Bodden's
house, dangling her bare feet in the salty water, she waited on the
small fish that she knew she would soon catch. With her mind
leading her to the fishermen's conversations, she was once again
in deep thought about her island and its people.

Because the island of Utila had little to offer in the line of work,
many husbands and fathers would leave the island for sometimes
a year at a time, seeking work in other countries around the world

for the betterment of their families. Such families reaped a greater-than-normal status for the children. These families' new and already-made clothing, shoes, and the likes were easily recognizable, for such ready-made garments were not available to the average kid.

 Yet each child, rich or poor, was happy in their own child-like way.

Monetary allowances for children were unheard of, as the children were content just to go to bed at night with a full tummy, which was not always so for all, as was the case of the little girl.

Breakfast mainly consisted of a slice of homemade coconut bread and a cup of coffee given to any kid who liked it at breakfast time. At times a fried green plantain - a favorite among the islanders - was added, along with refried red beans left over from the day before. This made for a fine meal. Oatmeal was also enjoyed, but not by little Faye. She was not an oatmeal lover like her sister Muriel, who would prop one leg up in a position known only to her while she enjoyed the slimy stuff.

The making of coffee was a laborious chore of putting logs into the wood-burning stove and building a fire to boil a kettle of water that was then poured over the coffee grounds. The brown liquid would drip through a homemade coffee bag made of cotton fabric that was sewn around a wire circle with a handle, which would then be held over a blue granite coffee pot as eager eyes watched and waited for the dripping to stop.

On occasion, eggs were a meal option, but usually they were sold for five cents each or exchanged for much more needed items, such as sugar.

With such common hardness of life, as one would call it, the little girl was still a content child, for though life was hard, it was still good.

Being pulled back from her daydreaming by the tugging of her fishing line, the little girl excitedly pulled her fish to the dock's safety. One by one, she pulled them until she had enough for the family's evening meal.

Note: If one knows no other way of life, then to one it is normal, for many times hardships are only in the mind if one becomes lazy to such daily tasks of performing one's obligations.

Section 3

A PLAYFUL ACCOUNT

Raking the yard the following day was not among Faye's favorite chores, for the rake that she used held an unpleasant memory. It was one made from sticks bunched together and tied securely to an old broom handle. This was what her mother had ordered from Mr. Clayton Bush and given to her as a birthday present.

With the raking finished and the day behind her as darkness was making its presence known, she jumped from the squeaking swing on the porch in search of friends who came together to play games in the cool, sandy street in front of their homes or the corner.

The street was barely lit by the dull light on the street poles, which at times were lit and at times were not, for the island of

Old Utila Corner Street Scene.

Utila was dependent upon the one generator that was housed in the town center in a tiny house of its own. This generator supplied a few hours of electricity at night whenever the mood would hit it to actually work. Upon failure, kerosene lamps were readily available.

The breezes blowing upon the children from the nearby ocean was a welcomed feeling of coolness as they played such famous games of hopscotch, marbles, and other island-invented child's games, of which some were scary to the children, but which they desired to play over and over again.

Such a scary one was called Miss Jenny Jones. Who Miss Jenny Jones was or where she came from, the children never knew. It was a simple game invented long ago by someone that I suppose we will never know. It began simply with the kids all sitting on the front steps while one of them was 'it.' 'It' would say "I come to see Miss Jenny Jones and how she is today." The end result was that Miss Jenny Jones was sick, then dead, then rotting. And then she was up your steps, then in the house, then under your bed. Miss Jenny Jones had came back to haunt all the island kids. Then, when 'it' said that she was under your bed, all the kids on the steps would run as fast as they could so that 'it' couldn't catch them and carry them to Miss Jenny Jones!

After the exhausted running and hiding, a drink of 'wata,' as the islanders called it, was required to cool thirsty throats.

It was such a silly but fun and exciting game. Such was the innocence of all the island kids to believe that Miss Jenny Jones was coming to get them!

With children scattering in all directions as they ran from Miss Jenny Jones, hollering voices of mothers could be heard as they gave the ringing calls for kids to head home for the night.

Note: Be it shameful for any parent to deprive their children from such innocence as one's childhood, for one must remember from whence they themselves came.

Section 4

THE HUMMINGBIRD

Faye, sitting in a dory by the lagoon

After a good night of sleep, little Faye once again was found in the family swing on the front porch of her home, singing at the top of her young voice. Sweet sounds of songs learned in church mixed with the squeaking sound of the swing's chain echoed to the ears of neighbors as she found tranquil peace in her small self.

Such tranquil peace was one day interrupted by Mrs. Ena Cooper as she made her way across her sandy yard, headed in the direction of the girl's house. Mrs. Ena asked Faye's mother if she would please quiet her hummingbird daughter because her daughter, Ena C., was at home and not feeling well and the hummingbird's singing was keeping her awake!

Such singing from the porch swing was a daily occurrence for the girl as she, with her child legs barely able to reach the floor, pushed the swing to its maximum.

Little Faye loved to accompany her mother and grandmother to what she referred to as 'The Old Ladies' Group.' On Monday nights, a group of ladies would gather at church for a time of fellowship and singing, followed by planning of up-coming events at which she was always present.

A favorite of hers was the sale of a concoction of shaved ice called the 'dry clem,' to which a red homemade plum syrup was added to make for a tasty treat. The girl would do the ice shaving from a large square block of ice using a hand-held shaver.

Following the planned events, Faye's mother would play the brown upright piano and, with windows swinging open, the singing voices would bellow out to listening ears in the street. A child's loud voice was easily detectable among those which belonged to different ladies known as Sisters Grace James, Pansy Bush, Oriella Brown, Hester Thompson, Lydia Bernard, Alva Jackson, Etna Morgan, Mae Wood, Frankie Cooper, and one they called Miss Pansy , along with her grandmother - Madeline Whitefield - and mother - Nonie Whitefield. From these practiced occasions of singing, Faye always found a great joy that would settle deep within her small being.

This joy so deep would soon be replaced by years of troubled interruptions to her young life. As of yet, the little girl would not know of the awaiting and dreaded changes that would come her way, disrupting her peaceful and simple self and her way of life as she knew it. She would face years of life on the neighboring islands of Roatan and Barbarat, with Barbarat being totally uninhabited by human beings.

Note: Far be it from any human, young or old, to complain of one's surroundings when one has no other choice. As for the obedience to parents of the child, be they young or old, one should always be ready to perform one's obligation and contribution to the one who gave them life.

Section 5

PORCHES, BIG EARS, WATCHING EYES, AND THE CAYS

Once the singing was over in her mode of daydreams, little Faye was again seeing pictures in her mind of her island and the way it was.

On the island of Utila, most of the colorful painted wooden homes stood high in the air on posts. The majority had front porches and swings where there sat various visitors with big ears ready to listen to the latest gossip. Open downstairs areas were reserved for hammocks and relaxation of friendly visits. Windows and doors stayed open most all the time, making allowances for the ocean breezes to cool the homes.

To the islander, a porch swing and a hammock were as important as the house itself. For such expected visits among friends, the front porch was the place to be so that no one would miss what was happening with the people going up or down the street, for the eyes and ears were always tuned to the conversations of the passerby.

The islanders themselves were a very hospitable and kindhearted group of people who all had unique qualities of their own.

The swing was also the common place of courtship among young people, as Faye would discover in a few years. Young courtships were closely monitored by mothers for reputational protection of daughters because of the many listening ears and watchful eyes of the neighbors and passerby.

The islanders also relished in the enjoyment gleaned from such pets as talking and singing parrots, which were kept in cages at the open downstairs areas of the homes. One never knew when a parrot would whistle, laugh, or sing at a passerby. The parrots when talking and singing, carried the heavy accent of the Caribbean people themselves and spoke both the English and Spanish languages without training.

A favorite place of the little girl's was upon the small wooden bridge which overlooked the ocean on one side and a large lagoon on the other, where children and adults alike could be seen in paddling dories on either side. While children could be enjoying a time of fishing, the adults could be transporting harvested fruit, vegetables, or coconuts, or at times even large rocks which would be used for added access to the water's edge.

Little Faye would gaze out across the blue ocean as she looked upon the beautiful sunsets, which were a joy for her young eyes to behold and which again placed many an imaginative scene in her young mind.

She would look to the west at the tiny cay nestled on the open ocean just a short distance away, yet far enough that the eyes could not see the relatives who lived there, such as Rebecca Diamond, Leo and Lena Diamond, and many more scattered throughout.

The small cay is surrounded by the most beautiful aquamarine ocean that the eye will ever see and where the children are all skilled swimmers. The reef that encompasses the tiny place can almost be touched, as it even comes to some of the people's back doors!

Even though the people of the cay have no iron shore of their own, they enjoy a favorite kind of seafood that comes from the iron shore of Utila. The iron shore - a favorite place to the little girl - housed the whelk, or sea snail. The whelks were large in size and would attach themselves to the hardened lava rocks underneath the water's surface, making it a danger to venture the climb over the black, jagged, and sharp-pointed steel volcano rocks to retrieve such seafood as the whelk. But the little girl, on many occasions accompanied by her Aunt Joy, did just a thing as this, for the need for such food was a must regardless of the danger. If one would encounter such a fall into that region of the island's ocean, the danger of being pulled under by heavy currents and smashed against the jagged rocks was a certainty. As sunken

Utila's Iron Shore

treasure would tell, many a vessel met its doom as it was pushed by large, rough waves onto the hard-pointed, steel-like rocks of the iron shore, crashing and spilling its precious treasure to the ocean's bottom.

Yet it's the most beautiful of all sights to stand at the beachside and look at the rough blue-and-turquoise sea where pirate and explorer vessels of long ago tried to cast anchor, hungry for the island's refuge. Standing at the site, one can't help but picture the historic accounts of Christopher Columbus and how he must have felt as he discovered, for himself, these Bay Islands of Honduras.

 Note: It should matter not who in this life would make discoveries, for one is not above the other. When a new discovery is excitedly made, be it large or small, then to the discoverer it becomes an achievement to the betterment and enjoyment of one's life.

Section 6

THE BREAD, BUTTER, AND CHEESE

After the daydreams on the bridge and a hard day of chores, little Faye was again wrapped tight in a white sheet waiting for sleep to claim her eyes. By the cock-a-doodle sound of a rooster mistakenly crowing at the rising of a full moon, the little girl peacefully slept as pleasant dreams of her childhood events filled her mind.

Butter; wonderful butter. At times the girl's mother would spare five cents and send her to her Aunt Trudy's and Foster Cooper's small general store in the neighborhood. It was at that small store that little Faye would stand at the counter on her tiptoes waiting on Fotee to serve her their order of the precious five cent piece of butter, or 'butta' as the islanders called it. The butta consisted of a small cut of about ¼ inch from what we know today as a stick of butter. Fotee had a special cutting technique. He would make absolutely certain that not one slip of his dull knife would cut away more than what was considered a five cent piece of butter. With the butta in hand, the girl would excitedly run home to the coconut bread that was waiting. That five cent piece then had to butter the bread for all of them!

Fotee was also the world's best 'thin slice of cheese' slicer! Using the same dull knife, he was mindful of his cutting technique. When Faye's mother would send her to buy a ten cent slice of cheese which had to be shared with the family, she would watch

Fotee slice the big round cheese, her mouth drooling in the hopes that he would this time cut it a little thicker... yet with no luck. No one was getting anything past Fotee! That slice of cheese was a welcomed sight to the family's humble table.

At times Faye would be given a ten cent coin to run back to the same store to purchase her own supper, a wonderful sweet bun sandwich. She would again watch as Fotee would slice open the sweet bun. He would then spread a thin layer of yellow mustard, followed by a thin slice of yellow cheese, slapping it between the sweet bun's folds. Wrapping it in paper was not necessary, as a hungry little Faye was waiting on it and it never made it out the store's door! The little girl would then long for an extra five cent coin that would buy a Coca-Cola with which to down the delicious bun sandwich. But something as simple as an added Coca-Cola was mostly afforded to the better-off people. However, to complain was unnecessary, as life was still good.

Fotee was a gentle soul, for if one didn't have available money for purchases he would extend a line of credit without asking anything in return. Such kindness was shown by all of the store owners to the islanders.

As little Faye would get older, at times when her Aunt Trudy and Fotee had to make a trip to the mainland, they would leave her to attend the little store and see to the people's needs. From the occasions of watching Fotee and his cutting techniques, she would catch herself doing the very same thing.

Note: The mind is an ever-learning tool and one can easily master any skill as long as there is a willing participant residing within the mind of the individual.

Section 7

THE MAKING OF COCONUT BREAD

Awakened by the cock-a-doodle wakeup call of a rooster crowing, this time at the rising of the sun, Faye headed to the kitchen in search of coffee and coconut bread. The coconut bread had to be made again today, as this was a daily occurrence in some households and a chore which required her help, as she was reminded today by her mother.

The making of coconut bread was a lengthy process within itself.

To make the bread, the coconuts first had to be picked from the tall trees, some of which Faye would often climb. To reach the coconuts, one had to be a skilled climber; otherwise, a fast downward sliding to the tree's rough trunk would cause an unpleasant burning sensation from injury to the chest. To peel away the thick, fibrous husk of the coconut, one had to use a coconut husker. This husker was made from a strong tree limb and carved with a sharp point, after which it was pounded deep into the ground with the sharp point facing upward and with finished results extending upward about three feet tall. Such a contraption would remain as it was for years to come. By a special technique known to the islander, the large coconut would then forcefully be jammed onto the pointed end time after time until all of the husk was torn away, thus exposing the brown shell of the coconut. The skilled use of a machete was then employed to chip away the hard brown coconut's shell.

The little girl had become a real pro at both techniques. Not a tear or rip in the flesh of the coconut could be seen from the forceful chops of her machete, yet never once was injury caused to her small hands or fingers. Such were the proficiencies of the islanders, including the little girl.

To extract the milk from the coconut, the fruit had to be grated. A homemade tin grater that fit perfectly in the dish pan was used. If one wasn't careful, the grater would grate more than just coconut, for such was a dangerous contraption. But it was a necessary skill to their way of life and one in which little Faye was already experienced.

Hot water was added to the grated coconut, which was then hand-squeezed in order to extract the milk. The dry, milk-less coconut, which to the islanders was called 'coconut trash,' was then fed to the chickens.

So were the lengthy preparations of the beginning stages of the making of coconut bread on a daily basis.

The coconut bread was so wonderful that when a layer of sweet homemade guava or mango jam was added, one could make an entire meal of it. To the islander, this also made for a before-bed treat to parents and children alike.

Note: When one is hungry, it should become a willingness on the part of the human race to fill such a void by whatever edible means available, be it sweet or bitter.

Section 8

AUNTS, COUSINS, SWEET BUNS, AND LASHINGS

Following the laborious chore of bread making and gathering firewood, it was time for a well-deserved break, which would include waiting on cousins who were asking for swimming permission from their mother, Aunt Eva Whitefield. Such a break had a costly effect.

After the swimming and baths were over, Faye would return to Aunt Eva's, only to watch her cousin Vermon take a lashing for helping himself to one of his mother's sweet rolls, which had already been counted and were ready to be delivered and sold to the store. Frightful and trembling and edging farther and farther away from the crime scene, she watched as her cousin's small legs jumped up and down, trying to avoid making contact with the hard belt. She stared at the scene before her, wondering who could be next, for as of yet Aunt Eva wasn't aware that two of the sweet rolls were missing!

With a planned run in her mind, she paused and tried to think of just what would be the easiest way to handle this situation. It didn't take but a fleeting moment before her tiny fleeing feet could be heard racing to find the door as she exited the kitchen of torture! To the islander parent, such lashings were a common punishment to misbehaving or hard-headed children.

Faye's mother, along with her Aunts Eva and Joy, baked coconut bread and sweet buns to be sold. Of course, the baking had to be done in a wood-burning stove. Such bread and buns were counted for precise sales. The baker was dependent upon the store owner for the pay that the counted goods would bring.

Of course, the shoppers all had their own favorite bread choices. While some would like her aunts', others would like her mother's. Each lady's baked goods had a different shape and size that made for easily recognizable orders.

These were hard-working women who saw to their families' needs to the fullest. Faye's mother would have four children of her own, as would her Aunt Joy, while her Aunt Eva would have eight.

With that being said, there were many little cousinly mouths to be fed from the sale of that bread, so the counted goods were off limits as in-between meal treats to little hungry bellies.

It was behind her Aunts' houses at the ocean's edge that the little girl passed many happy hours with friends and cousins. Behind Aunt Eva's house there was a deep swimming hole where the salty water was cooler than normal. This was a favorite swimming place to neighborhood kids. Behind Aunt Joy's house was an old half-sunken boat which had made ground long ago, but which made a perfect play place for swimming, jumping, and fishing.

Other favorite swimming places were at Fotee's, Capt. Junny Cooper's, and Miss Tonia's docks. All the kids referred to those docks as such. It would be from these docks, which were in the girl's neighborhood, that they would jump in the water and play for hours on end.

It would be from Fotee's dock that the girl's brother, Gilbert, one day pushed her into the deep water and told her to swim or drown! It was a custom that island kids learned to swim at an early age to avoid drowning, which was almost unheard of on the island. Such was the method of some for teaching one to swim, for it was a must that the children learn. Such methods were passed down from generation to generation by the islanders.

Note: When a person, be they child or adult, knows no other way of life, then to them they have missed nothing.

Section 9

MEMORIES FROM THE PAST

After the fast getaway from the 'kitchen of torture' and while sitting on a limb at the top of a large almond tree with a small bag of green mangoes and a little salt wrapped in a chunk of paper, little Faye found refuge from the sting of the belt's cracking noise.

This particular almond tree was among her favorite places to be. She enjoyed the sneakiness of information gained from people as they passed below the tree in which she sat as soft giggles escaped her lips.

Another enjoyment of the girl in the tree was when she would take her mind back to funny and interesting things that came her way, as they so often did.

One of such things was her father's sister, Aunt Joy , and her love for Coca-Cola. At times when Faye was lucky enough to get one of her own Coca-Colas, she would keep a close watch for Aunt Joy! If her aunt was anywhere close by, she always asked for a sip of the precious, cold, dark fluid. Aunt Joy's sip was a very long one that caused the girl's eyes to mark where the precious fluid was both before and after the lengthy sip. Aunt Joy always followed that sip by saying "Aaah!" which the little girl did not understand at the time. Life was still happy and good even though the bottle was half empty!

Feeding milk to the kids on an everyday basis was unheard of, yet somehow they all grew teeth strong enough to open anything and everything! But if you were one of Eula and Ellis Morgan's kids, you could have your fill of milk, for they raised cattle and sold the milk.

Once, after a heated game of marbles with the marble champion, Miss Eula's daughter Dottie, Faye and the young girl were standing in Miss Eula's kitchen. Great pots of milk sat on the stove cooling down from the heated temperature, having already formed a layer of thick cream on top. The girl's fingers, along with Dottie's, would make a swift rake through the delicious cream! Upon being caught, the girls would be hollered at by Miss Eula, who would say "You two shes betta ge outta heh" as she ran them both from the kitchen.

Even though the children's teeth were all strong, like what happens to all kids, they all took turns losing them. If one of them needed a dentist, they all pulled each other's teeth, as long as they were already loose. Dentists on the island of Utila were limited to one old man for the more serious cases. But before visiting him, potions were first tried and tested on the children by parents or neighbors. The kids had their own favorite people to whom they would go to have their shaky teeth pulled, or even to have splinters removed, which required a steady hand.

Earaches were a nightmare to the little girl. When an earache would attack, a chunk of cotton dipped in hot coconut or castor oil was stuffed into the ear with little sympathy to follow.

Another memorable and painful occurrence was the all-too kid-famous occurrence of stepping on a nail, better known to the islander as a 'nail jugg.'

Since doctors to the island were few and far between visits, they had to deal with their own methods of treatments, for there were no hospitals.

The treatment for that rusty nail pierce to the foot was a chunk of coconut bread and half of a lime. The lime and bread were pressed against the injury and tied to the foot with a cloth to hold it in place while the kid limped around for days.

Such a thing as a tetanus injection was not available. Had it been available, the kid in question would never be brought from their hiding place, for the children fled from any doctor with a needle.

All the swimming kids at one time or another suffered the painful black spines of the sea urchin to their tiny feet, yet the cure for that didn't cost much - just a participant who was willing to urinate on your hurting, spine-filled foot! This treatment would kill the live spines and cause them to eventually exit the foot or be easily removed by neighborly, skilled hands holding a sharp needle.

Note: Greatly numbered are the childhood memories that one would bring back from the far recesses of one's mind, only to find some as pain and others as pleasure. Yet the combination of both is necessary to mold us into the unique individuals that we are today.

Section 10

PRECIOUS WATER

Hearing the hollering call of her mother, Faye scurried down from her hiding place in the almond tree, hoping that her mother's beckoning call was not for the cause for which she thought it could be. But she was right.

Even though today was the day that the washing was to be done, Faye knew that they had run out of water and had hoped that her mother had money to purchase it from Mr. Jacky Cooper, instead of Faye having to go in the canoe to get it from the public well across the island. Mr. Jacky would only charge a small amount of

Mr. Jacky Cooper, at Cola de Mico Well

money to fetch it from the well and deliver it in his wheelbarrow.

On the island of Utila, the thing that was needed most was fresh water, which everyone rich and poor alike had to acquire by the same means when there was no rain. Every household was dependent upon the rains to provide them with fresh water.

Most households had a wooden tank that was set high in the air on posts to house the water. Many of the people had asbestos tanks, as no one knew of the health risks of such tanks.

Spouts made from tin were attached to the housetops and allowed to hang over the tanks to catch the rain water, which was housed for long periods without treatment. One would think it hazardous to their health, but the mind is a great tool of acceptance to the body when it has to be. If a water tank wasn't achievable then water was housed and held in tin barrels.

At the first sound of thunder or the blackness of a rain cloud, the women - never the men - would go about hurriedly gathering barrels and buckets, placing them underneath the various spouts to catch the precious water. The water in those tanks had to be rationed to last until the next rains.

Drinking water was never treated with anything to ensure safe drinking, yet somehow they all got through that as well.

A welcomed bit of fun to neighborhood kids came during the rainy season.

Little Faye's Grandmother Madeline didn't have the common wooden tank, but a cement cistern provided to her by money sent home from her sons who left the island in search of work.

It was at this time of heavy rains that her grandmother would plan for a cistern cleaning. The cleaning consisted of the kids climbing into the cistern and scrubbing away the green slime from the walls while playing and splashing around in the cool fresh water. The cement cistern kept the water cooler than normal.

The girl's family's drinking water was kept in a large, round, Indian clay jug referred to as the 'water cooler.' This water cooler sat on a shelf near the kitchen window with a dipping water ladle floating on the inside, readily available for whoever needed a cool drink of fresh water. The family led a simple life, but to the girl that water cooler was a welcomed sight after a day of running around the island or climbing trees.

Note: One should never measure a simple life as a failure, for it is meant to be enjoyed by all fortunate enough to breathe the breath of life given by its creator.

Public well where Faye drew water from.

Section 11

GRANDMA'S TORTURE BAG

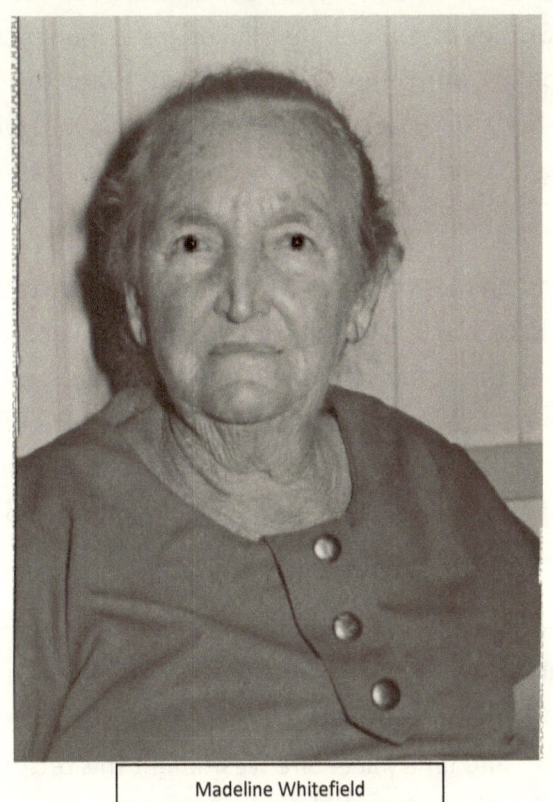

Madeline Whitefield

With the washing now complete, the clothes - lined in orderly perfection upon the clothesline - blew in the island breeze, sending out their fresh-washed scent which signaled that the day's chores were over.

When her tummy grumbled in pain from eating too many green mangoes and normal attempts failed to ease the pain, little Faye's Grandmother Madeline was called. This caused the girl to tremble in fear, for she well remembered her grandmother's form of treatment for a rumbling belly filled with green mangoes. The grandmother would administer treatment from the dreaded torture bag, which was her answer for what she called a 'wormy belly.' On the island, such wormy bellies were common to children, for they often took their fill of green mangoes, guavas, almonds, plums, and other unwashed fruit. When the little girl would see her grandmother walking across the yard with the torture bag in hand there was only one word that came to mind... RUN!

The bag was a pinkish color and made of rubber. Attached to one end was a long, black, hard tube with holes throughout. The bag was huge - to the point that it held one gallon of water! The water exited through the holes in the long black tube. This was the enema bag. After administration, little Faye would name it the 'enemy bag,' for once administered a kid really had no choice but to run from such an enemy.

To treat the same 'worminess,' the girl's mother, on the other hand, would make for each of the kids a twelve-ounce tumbler under the full moon. This juice consisted of Epsom salt mixed with water, sugar, and lime juice. She was taught this recipe by the same grandmother who administered the 'enemy bag,' Madeline Whitefield. Her mother would set glasses of the awful liquid on a shelf near the kitchen window and tell the children that they had to down it all before the setting of the sun that day!

Note: Any parent or grandparent who would seek treatment to aid their ailing child should be regarded as good. And one's treatment of administration learned from generations past, be it strange or not, should never be judged as long as it contributes to one's health.

Section 12

THE TWO IRONS

With her grandmother's 'torture bag' now put away until needed again and with the grumbling belly back to normal, little Faye watched as her mother 'cooked' the clothes in a thick, hot liquid. 'Cooking the clothes' was what the little girl called the method of starching, a process of adding powdery starch to boiling water until thickened. The clothes were then dipped into the thick liquid and the excess starch was squeezed out, after which they were then hung on the clothesline to dry. After the clothes were dried they would become like a hardened and stiff sheet of glue, unable to blow in the island's breeze.

Ironing the clothes was a must. Faye's mother always made sure that the family's clothes were nicely pressed. Most of the time, the pressing was done by the girl.

At first the iron that was used was one that was made of actual iron. To get the iron hot, it had to be put on top of the wood-burning stove and wiped clean of any soot. It ironed barely one garment before it got cold again and the entire process had to be repeated, as it would over and over again. This process took several hours to complete. This sort of iron was common to the islanders.

Eventually they would upgrade to a fancy kerosene iron. Now they were getting somewhere. After the kerosene was poured into the little holding tank of the iron it had to be pumped up. The iron was then lit with a match in the special lighting area of the iron. This one held the heat much longer than the iron one.

Many days, little Faye performed such chores on a hungry belly that had to wait until mealtime before it would be filled... and at times just partially filled. But to the girl, ripe almonds on the trees would calm the grumbling and hungry growl of her belly.

Note: One should always be content with the means which are common to one's life, for to complain is seldom a good contribution to society.

Section 13

ABANDONED AND A WEDDING

Little Faye, now happy and free from any and all chores for the day, faced her first day of real anger. Disillusioned and angry, the little girl ran crying to her special hiding place at the top of her almond tree. The day had come that her young world was shaken and ripped away from under her.

Her father had decided that he no longer wished to live with the family. Up to this point he had been the provider for the household, along with help from the sales of her mother's coconut bread. He left his family on Utila to work on another island where his brother, Richard Whitefield - known as Dickie - was working harvesting coconuts.

The island was referred to by the locals as Barbarat, but to the Spanish and foreigners it was called Barbareta. Barbarat was a beautiful island where jade could be seen along its white sandy beaches. The jade would wash down from the hills to the beaches during heavy rains or storms. Faye's Uncle Dickie's family made visits to Barbarat during the school off season. The island of Barbarat was totally uninhabited by humans other than her uncle's family.

As the months passed, eventually the girl and her mother and sometimes her sister, would go to Barbarat to stay for long periods at a time. They would share a small wooden house with the girl's Uncle Dickie, Aunt Mary, and cousins. All the kids hated it there and wanted to go home to Utila to their playmates.

It was also at this time that Faye's father decided to father more children at the nearby settlement of Helene, as it was called by the locals. It was known to the Spanish and foreigners as Helena.

Things were not working between Faye's mother and father at all, yet they would continue to live on the island in isolation for a time. This isolation worked hard against the little girl.

Later on, she and her mother and sister would head back home to Utila. Her father would make periodic visits back to Utila and stay for a day or two. These visits then grew fewer and further between until eventually they stopped all together. It would seem that his devotion was to his new family in Helene.

It was at this time that Faye's older sister Sadie would marry a man from the island of Roatan. At eight years old and dressed in her fluffy blue flower girl dress with a white ribbon holding her red curls in place, the little girl dropped petals of island flowers from her blue basket down the aisle of the church's floor. That very same night, the new bride left her island home of Utila with her husband. The husband, Henry Jackson, would take her away to live on his island home of Roatan.

Faye's family, now left without the provisions of her father, was facing difficult times. Life for her and her mother, sister, and brother changed drastically. With no income, her mother was forced to take the lead in raising the kids as best she could, but was happy to do so.

Many days they made their meals from fish that the girl's Uncles Jake Hal and Sheldon would give to them.

Her mother worked hard and became a favorite seamstress for the entire island for making everything from fine layette baby clothes to bridesmaid dresses.

Both Faye and her sister Muriel were educated in the art of fine embroidery stitching at an early age. It would fall to the two of them to do the fine stitching which served as an added touch to the baby clothes that their mother so handsomely produced with pride, yet without a pattern. There was no garment worn by male or female that she could not produce by her old peddle-foot black iron Singer sewing machine; the very same machine on which the girl would learn to sew. Faye's mother could create something out of nothing and was not afraid of hard work, for such a spirit was in her ancestral roots.

Note: Hardships that come to individuals should become lessons well-learned, for in learning such lessons a repeat of such can be avoided.

Section14

CINDERELLA AND SANTA CLAUSE

Edwin Jackson's store, where the bread was sold.

Making her exit down from the almond tree, little Faye had no choice but to fulfill her daily chores. Each day except on Sundays, the for-sale coconut bread which Faye's mother baked had to be delivered to the store. It would become her job to carry the large sack of warm coconut bread flung over her shoulder as she made her deliveries on foot to Mr. Edwin Jackson's general store that was located in the downtown corner of town. One expense of this chore was being laughed at by her sister Muriel and her friends as they repeatedly called her Santa Clause.

Her greatest embarrassment came from passing the boys on whom she had crushes. She felt shameful allowing them to see her carrying that heavy sack of bread flung over her shoulder.

Hiding was out of the question, as everyone on the island knew who everyone was and the hiding place would be revealed by the onlooker. With the option to hide being out of the question, she would continue down the street with the heavy sack of bread.

Scrubbing the floors also fell under the girl's list of chores. Faye didn't understand why scrubbing the floors had to be done in this particular form.

First, she would have to search under the coconut trees for a dried coconut that was still in its husk - the outer house which encased the coconut with its brown, hard shell hidden on the inside. She would cut off the bottom end of the large coconut to about four inches in length. That would become her scrubbing tool - the tough fibers made for a rough, steel-like tool!

Coconut Scrubber

Water was then thrown over the floor with soap added to create a foamy mess. The girl then positioned her tool under one foot and extended her leg in a back-and-forth motion, scrubbing away at the invisible dirt that may or may not have been on the kitchen floor. This was the custom of the islanders to keep the floors clean. It's no wonder that the painted floors never stood a chance against such a weapon as the dreaded coconut-head scrubber!

After the scrubbing at nothing, water was then poured over the floor again and swept out the door with a broom.

This was done every Saturday before the swimming privileges were allowed and while swimming friends eagerly waited on swimming buddies to finish such chores.

But where Faye's sister, Muriel, was concerned she never did see her scrubbing those floors. She always somehow managed to escape that. I suppose that one could even call her ability to escape smart on her part.

This was the way of life to the islanders, for they knew no other way. Such is the case all over this globe, with each group having their own way of life.

Note: Intelligence comes in many different packages and one should always be seen seeking it.

Section 15

BROTHER, MONEY, AND FIRECRACKERS

The end result of being abandoned by their father was Faye's brother leaving the island in search of work which would take him to faraway places around the world. Faye, in her place of solitude and saddened as goodbyes were said, would weep for his presence. The two were as close as any siblings could be.

Her brother would then send money home to help the family in their time of crisis. The money received from him was a welcomed sight and was stretched to the fullest to meet the many needs of his family. It would become Faye's job to go to the small and

Utila's Credit Union.

simple wooden building of the Utila credit union located on Cola de Mico Road. It was there that the precious money would be passed over to her by Mr. Keith Morgan.

To Faye's brother, Gilbert Donaldson Whitefield, your sister Faye thanks you and you have her love and respect, for without you life itself would have been much tougher on all of us.

Faye's brother Gilbert Donaldson Whitefield

By then the girl's sister Muriel had also found work as a clerk at Mr. Frank Morgan's general store. The small earnings saw to her needs and wants that otherwise would have been difficult to manage.

Mr. Frank Morgan's store was an immediate neighbor to the store of Mr. Archie Henderson. At Christmastime Little Faye, along with friends, would make purchases of firecrackers, chasers, matches, and sparklers from Mr. Archie's store.

The streets would be filled with the cracking sounds of the loud bangs of firecrackers as they spread their colorful, windblown paper through the air and carried away, dropping it on various parts of the smoke-filled, sandy streets. The children and adults both would then scatter in all directions trying to outrun the chasers, but most were unable to do so.

Such were great times to the little girl, as Christmastime brought with it such fun-filled nights of street play which would be followed by a quick visit to Mr. Franky's.

Note: Pleasant memories of one's childhood should be protected and guarded, for they can never be replaced or easily forgotten.

Section 16

CARRIED AWAY TO ROATAN ISLAND

It was not long after the fun of Christmas and firecrackers that little Faye would encounter a drastic change to her young life.

The eight-year-old girl was excitedly packing her few cotton dresses and other necessary items for a short trip by stuffing them into a small, weather-beaten suitcase. Her excitement came from the chance to see her sister again after months of separation. It was now time that the family paid a visit to her married sister and her husband on Roatan Island, which was around thirty or so miles away.

The normal mode of transportation between the islands was either by dory or small cargo boats, which made slow speed upon the sea. The trip could take as long as three to four hours of enduring the rough, open sea.

She and her mother and sister would board a small boat called *Bonnie J* belonging to Mr. Albert Jackson of Roatan. It was captained by her sister's husband, Capt. Henry Jackson, brother to Albert Jackson. *Bonnie J* carried the name of Albert and Eileen Jackson's firstborn daughter.

The *Bonnie J*'s reason for coming to Utila was to bring fuel from Mr. Albert Jackson to Mr. Frank Morgan for distribution among the locals. Mr. Morgan had a very large silver tank close to the dock where the boat would make port.

It was on one of the *Bonnie J*'s return trips back to Roatan that they would make their journey with a great barge being towed behind.

That day the ocean was extremely rough and steaming was slow as the family endured what seemed like ten or more hours on the open sea surrounded by the nauseating smell of fuel. The combination of tossing waves and overwhelming fumes was having such great effect upon the passengers that they hugged the outside rail of the boat for the need to vomit. This occurred over and over, until finally a long island outline was spotted.

As they neared the channel of French Harbour, boats could be seen at various docks and houses that lined the ocean's edge as children played in the salty water.

At last, landfall was made at the dock of Albert Jackson as crew members of *Bonnie J* threw ropes to onlookers and the boat was securely tied to the dock. Little Faye, her mother, and sister now wobbled with ocean wave drunkenness as they walked the distance to her sister's house. The girl missed nothing as her eyes followed and looked all around, seeing what she could see and placing the pictures in her mind for later use.

Upon reaching her sister's home, little Faye was happy to see that there was a front porch with a swing. It would be during conversations held on this porch that she would learn more about the island of Roatan.

The island of Roatan is a beautiful one with multiple high-rolling, green hills. The island was somewhere in the vicinity of 44 kilometers in length and just over 4 kilometers in width. Roatan also sits on the largest barrier reef in the Western Hemisphere and is sought by divers from around the world.

At this time the town of French Harbour was a clean, quiet, and quaint place where people moved about its streets on foot and where churches were a wonderful place of gathering to its people, as they were for all the Bay Islands.

The church's doors and windows stayed open during services. Beautiful singing could be heard great distances away without the use of microphones, for such was the strength of the peoples' voices.

Little Faye was not a stranger to these churches and neither was her singing voice.

The windows and doors being open made for a good option for those who preferred to observe from the outside. Once each year, late on New Year's Eve, those same onlookers would present themselves - handsomely dressed - only to be seen reverently seated on the inside pews! This too was a custom to all the Bay Islands.

Note: Cultural freedom should be embraced when it is made available, for doing so lends to the enjoyment of one's existence.

Section 17

LEFT BEHIND

Little Faye was packed, excited, and ready for her return back to Utila. She wondered about the looks exchanged between her mother and her married sister. What the little girl did not know was that the return home would not include her. It was then that once again her world was turned upside down as her young life suddenly took a turn for the worse, for her mother had decided that she was to be left behind to live with her sister Sadie. Since her sister's husband was a boat captain and was gone to sea for weeks or sometimes months at a time, her sister needed someone who could stay with her. This decision changed the little girl's happy world. The change for her at that time was not good, as disillusionment once again found its way into her young life.

Standing at Mr. Albert Jackson's dock and watching the small boat pull away, little Faye waved final goodbyes to her mother and sister, but it was more than her little self could take. Finding a hiding place behind one of the large Texaco fuel tanks, the little girl gave way to her tears of despair.

As would any child of eight years, she did her plentiful share of crying over the next several months, for she longed for the only home that she had ever known - Utila. As much as a child could know hate, she hated Roatan Island simply because her heart was at home in Utila with family and friends, where she was used to running all over the island at will. She lived in a torment of homesickness.

Her sister, now her mother, on many occasions would send her to Mr. Albert Jackson's store, located in the downtown area of French Harbour. As she waited on Miss Eileen to fill the shopping list, Miss Eileen sometimes rewarded her with a candy bar called 'Zero.' This precious lady was a true friend to the girl's sister and was loved and respected throughout the island. Miss Eileen Jackson was rarely seen without a smile upon her beautiful face. On many occasions, little Faye would accompany her sister for visits to Miss Eileen's home that was located next to her store. After the candy bars, the shopping became very interesting to the girl.

She would also often be sent to another store belonging to Albert and Henry's father, Mr. Darvin Jackson. His small grocery store sat near a canal that had a small wooden bridge running across to the next side. Upon these visits, Mr. Darvin would at times compliment little Faye by giving her a free Coca-Cola, but not before saying "Here old bee, this one's on me." 'Old bee' is what the people of Roatan would call the people of Utila, but the people of Utila never knew why.

The child hate that she had for Roatan was now somewhat diminishing. With Utila still in her blood, she still made it a point to walk around the more desolate areas of French Harbour in search of such adventures to which she was accustomed.

She would soon find pleasure within a slingshot, which was not so fortunate for the pigeons due to its deadly force.

To get to her intended target area she first had to pass by the homes of Miss Orella and Anna Dixon, where she would later spend time with friends.

Strolling slowly along the dense and bushy narrow path and getting close to the pigeons' hiding place where they would be feasting upon white berries, little Faye was leery about passing Mr. Egga's - as they called him – small, unpainted, wooden house that was almost hidden among the island's foliage. The girl was afraid of the old man just as she had always been afraid of other old men in Utila who carried crocus sacks flung over their shoulders. This fear was etched in her mind, as it was common for parents, when scolding a child, to tell them that such old men would put them in their sack and leave with them if they didn't behave! Strolling to this section of the dense area always made her feel closer to the home that she stilled missed.

Over the course of time the little girl, now growing up, would also find other areas of interest. Such an area was near her sister's house, where a boat was being built. The boat belonged to Mr. Robert Arch and would be named *Diez Años*. Many days would find her seated nearby on a log or rock, watching the wooden structure that was now taking the form of a boat. Most of the Jackson brothers – Albert, Henry, Errol, and Spencer - would also be lending a hand to the building of the boat, while others such as Mr. Paul Dixon could be seen at times hammering away. Needless to say, the girl was present on the day that the boat would be rolled upon logs and pulled with ropes as she made her first descent to the water. Faye, at this time, was being treated by the entire Jackson family as one of their very own little ones.

Eventually she would make friends with some girls, as she was now experiencing different stages of 'growing up.' These girls included Emma, Olene, Susie, Stella, and Laura Dixon, Donna Thompson, and Bobbilene - better known as A. A - and Sherry Arch. These friendships would blossom in the coming years during

Faye (Third row, top left) and her friends at French Harbour Church of God.

school hours, for they all attended the same schools taught by Misses Vera, Betty and Lola. These same friends would sometimes tease her and call her 'old bee.'

The dialects of the two islands were a bit different. Whereas the Utila people would refer to a crowd as 'among you,' the Roatan people would refer to the same as 'you all.' Yet both would pronounce these phrases with heavy island accents. Faye would then get teased by these friends as they also called her 'among you.'

Little by little, she would make slow progress at adjusting to her new life. She still missed Utila and being able to run to her favorite places, but above all she missed her almond tree and its yellow fruit.

With Roatan being so much larger than Utila, walking around the island was limited. This island had other islets and cays that belonged to it, two of which were the islands of Barbarat and Helene, where her father was now living.

On a certain occasion, several of the young people including herself went on a short dory ride to a special swimming area. The group was headed to a favorite area which they referred to as 'between the two cays' in the area of French Cay. It was there that she was challenged by Hoyt Dixon to a swimming match. Hoyt said to Faye "Old bee, I bet I can beat you in a swimming race between the two cays." Needless to say, the girl couldn't resist the challenge, for Hoyt did not know of her Utila ocean training. As friendly eyes watched and hands clapped cheers of excitement, the race began. The practiced skills of her swimming days in Utila from Fotee's dock to Miss Tonia's gave her the lead. The old bee from Utila won the race! This was her very favorite memory of Hoyt Dixon.

During Faye's years growing up on Roatan, the highway between French Harbour and Coxen Hole was a curvy, unpaved, and dusty red clay road. The highway was called the 'Three S's' because of its numerous curves. There were just a few vehicles on French Harbour at that time, one of which belonged to Mr. Felix Bodden - better known as 'Mr. Finky.' The friends would pay a few cents to take rides in it, for to them it was a strange sight. Mr. Finky would drive them as far as Munky Apple Gully and then back. The young ones would exit the vehicle blabbering their excitement from such a ride.

Note: Friendships that become stronger as one becomes older must be safeguarded, for a true friend is not easily found.

Section 18

GROWING UP IN THE JACKSON FAMILY

Seated on the back of her brother-in-law's motorcycle, the girl and man set off for a trip along the three S's road that would lead them to Coxen Hole. It wasn't long before they took a nasty fall on the dusty, red road. Henry suffered a red face from the sheer embarrassment of it all, while Faye sustained just a few scratches and bruises.

One day, her sister Sadie announced that they were having a baby. That was good news to the young girl, for she always loved to be around babies. She couldn't wait for the little niece or nephew to arrive. One evening, she was made to spend the night at the home of her mother's friend, Mrs. Orella Dixon, who was also the mother to Faye's friends. The time had come for the baby to be born. On the islands, the babies were all born at home and any and all children living in the homes were shipped off to friends' or neighbors' until the event was over. The next day, Faye would be summoned back to the house to find a small bundle of a little, pink, wrinkly figure lying beside its mother. It was a boy, which they gave the name Andall Jackson. A couple of years later another baby would be born to them and given the name Dale Jackson.

The girl's life was getting better all the time. As the boys reached three years of age, Faye would take them in the evenings to play at the only swing set in French Harbor. It was privately owned by the wonderful Hyde family.

Mr. Albert Jackson, at that time, acquired a much larger boat called *Cheryl J*. This boat carried the name of Albert and Eileen's second daughter. The girl's brother-in-law, Capt. Henry Jackson, would become the *Cheryl J*'s captain. *Cheryl J* was used for transporting coconuts from Roatan to Tampa. During the return trips from Tampa, Henry would always bring special goods like clothing, shoes, candy, etc. for his wife, boys, and Faye. It was a time of great expectation as they awaited the docking of the *Cheryl J*.

Henry Jackson, Faye's 2nd dad.

Sometimes apples, pears, and grapes were also brought. This meant that Christmas was coming! These special fruit only made it to the islands at Christmastime.

One of the girl's most embarrassing memories was on one of those return trips when Henry brought her a really special gift. The gift was so special that it caused her to shy away from him for a time. It was an almost-teen-ready blue brassiere! The young girl was growing up and didn't even know it! She was innocent to the changes that life would bring her.

Another time, Henry brought her a chocolate-brown pair of ugly shoes! She hated those shoes and thought them extremely ugly! They were called Oxfords and reminded her of shoes that a very old man would wear and were the ugliest shoes she had ever seen in her young life. She would, however, find someone who liked them and bought them from her. That was a happy day!

As the years went by, Faye's mother and her sister Muriel would make frequent visits to Roatan, at times staying for weeks, spending time with the little boys, Andall and Dale.

The young girl was still homesick, but she no longer hated Roatan so much, for life had become much easier with some frills added to it. Such frills included candy bars, Coca-Cola, goods from the USA, and spending money.

Since the Jackson family, from the beginning, had adopted her as one of their very own kids, many times Uncle Albert - as she had been calling him - would hand her a piece of money as he rumpled her red, curly hair and called her by the famous 'old bee' name. The girl, from the time she was a small child, would learn to love this great Jackson family.

Note: The hardships and disappointments that one encounters in life are well-worth their trouble if they bring about a better knowledge of bonds not easily broken.

Section 19

THE BOYFRIENDS

At almost fourteen years old, Faye and her friends were now turning into nice-looking young ladies. As was customary to all the islands, the girls enjoyed taking nightly walks through the town. If one had a boyfriend, then the walks became even more interesting - especially when a darker-than-normal spot would be passed, for the young loves would steal a handhold or even a quick kiss if they thought that no one was watching.

The girls all had their favorite hang-out spots for milkshakes and the like, such as Miss Mabel's place.

Life for the young girl was much easier, for her sister Sadie would see to it that she always had a little spending money of her own. But at the same time, Sadie would give her a fit for her dress

French Harbour street scene where Faye and friends took walks.

being too short! Her sister would let down the hems of her dresses, but Faye would - without her knowledge - bring the hems back up again! On and on the battle would continue.

Walking through the town of French Harbour with friends was pleasant and memorable to the young girl. With the blue ocean just a stone's throw away and its heavy breezes blowing their hair about their faces was a loveliness that was soon to come.

Of course, there were admirers that would try to take walks with the girls and some that Faye never cared to have walk with her, for they would try to hold her hand or steal a kiss, which was forbidden. As of yet she had never been kissed. But of course, that was her choice. She had no problem with administering a quick slap to their hands or face and - on more than one occasion - she had done just that. After all, a girl had to protect her honor, even if the attempt was just for a handhold or kiss! Sometimes, to get away from the ones she did not like, she would make her escape to either of the nearby little stores and wait endlessly until the coast was clear!

As the friends would sometimes sit on a favorite cement sidewalk, a man they called 'Jo Jo' would keep them entertained as he played his guitar and sang "No Letters Today."

Life was getting interesting on Roatan Island, and it was getting good - that is, until she made a quick trip back to Utila for a visit. As it had always been her custom to go to her favorite places of isolation, on a particular day an unfortunate thing happened that would leave her traumatized for a long time to come.

Note: Many are the unfortunate things that would befall us, but to learn to live after is greater than the unfortunate things themselves.

Section 20

THE CHANGE

It was on the island of Roatan, during a nasty hurricane, that the fourteen-year-old was changed from girl to woman. The nearly Category 3 monster, named Francelia, was packed with heavy winds and rain and brought with it deadly claws of fury, making havoc of anything and everything in its path, spinning and turning until it found its way to the Bay Islands. The family, among others, evacuated to higher ground at the home of Mrs. Minnie Jackson. Mrs. Jackson's humble wooden home was seated upon a beautiful, high hill that overlooked almost the entire island.

Many days, the girl would go to this home to pick guavas from Mrs. Minnie's tree, only to find herself staring out to sea as she had done her entire life on her island home of Utila.

The day of the hurricane, many members of the Jackson family and their friends took shelter at Mrs. Minnie's home, as many had done in previous hurricanes. No one considered space, for the need of safety was foremost on everyone's mind.

The young girl, in her delicate condition of womanhood, was completely unprepared for this new challenge that she was facing alone. It was common for parents not to share much information on the subject. The girl only knew that, somehow, she had to handle her situation alone because there was no way that she was telling anyone - including her sister Sadie. It was not as memorable an occasion as it should be to any young woman.

The hurricane winds and rain beat heavily upon the little wooden house. She would find herself standing in ankle-deep water for hours as the rain and wind made havoc of the roof, causing damage to it. Upon twice being frightened - once by the hurricane and the other by her womanly condition - the girl didn't know what to do. Needless to say, she was a bundle of nerves; yet a secretly-kept bundle of nerves at that.

Some hours later, amidst the ankle-deep water, rain, and winds, she ventured out onto the small front porch of the house to think. She knew of the danger for such an action, but she was in trouble and needed answers. The young girl watched as the heavy winds and rain beat the green mangoes and guavas from off the trees, sending them soaring through the air like rocks from a slingshot. She watched as great mango trees buckled under the weight of the forceful winds. The winds were pulling her this way and that, but the need to think was greater than her own safety, which she never considered. Standing at the wooden, weathered porch rail and holding tight as it rocked her back and forth, the little porch gave way and she was thrown to the ground as a target for the wind and heavy rains. Who knows what would have happened had two hands not pulled her back to safety. The girl would never learn who that person was or was not.

Note: Along this journey called life, some things are best left to the wonderment of the mind, for what one proceeds to wonder is to be forever etched in the mind of the wonderer.

Section 21

DR. POLO GALINDO AND COXEN HOLE

Dr. Polo's residence and clinic on right, on Coxen Hole's main street.

The result of this fall was that a piece of the wooden rail became embedded in the girl's abdomen, where it would stay until a doctor could be seen in a few days. It was days before evacuated families were able to return to their homes. When the men would think it safe enough to venture out from their places of safety, they would go to various neighborhoods, checking any damages that may have been made to homes.

Hurricanes were no stranger to the Caribbean Bay Islands.

Once, as a small child on the island of Utila, the girl's family waited a little late before evacuating their home. The hurricane was nearer than anyone knew and the need to seek shelter was almost too late. By this time, the ocean's tide had made its presence known as families waded through the street, filled almost knee-deep with water. Walking at that point became very difficult, especially to the little ones. Suddenly, a sheet of tin from someone's roof came soaring through the air. Luckily, it missed them all as they trudged on, trying to reach safety.

On about day three, with the piece of wood still embedded into the girl's abdomen, Henry was able to get her to a local doctor. The only doctor in French Harbour at that time was Dr. Sturdy. They entered the small, humble clinic at the doctor's home, only to be told that Dr. Sturdy was someplace else on an emergency.

With just one option left, the two headed to see Dr. Polo Galindo in Coxen Hole. Henry put her on the back of his motorcycle to make the bumpy drive to Coxen Hole. The heavy rains and tree limbs and debris scattered everywhere made for a dangerous and nasty ride along the muddy Three S's Road. The pain from the infection that had set into the wound and surrounding flesh was severe. She silently prayed that they would not encounter another fall along Three S's Road. If one wasn't a careful driver along that red, muddy, clay road, they could easily meet their death, for the terrain below the high, mountainous, and curvy road was bottomless.

Once the drive smoothed out to make way for flatter ground, you could consider yourself entering Coxen Hole. It was a simple town of unpaved and dusty roads. Its streets were never empty, as folks were busily walking up and down as they went about their everyday business routines. Sidewalk sales of fruit, vegetables, and even readymade clothing - which was not common to the islands - could be seen for sale along the sidewalks. Children played in neighboring yards without fear of danger whatsoever, such as on all the Bay Islands. Like the rest of the islands, the town of Coxen Hole was near the ocean's edge. Boats either delivering or picking up goods from the mainland or one of the other islands could be seen at the dock of Mr. Henry Warren, loading and unloading at any given time. People sat in the nearby park on cement benches, catching up on the latest news or gossip. The town itself made a pretty picture with its two-story homes and

Coxen Hole Park

Gathering place for visitors and locals alike.

balconies of decorative early French design. It brought to mind the style of early settlers to the islands.

The needs of Coxen Hole were many, but at the time the options were few. A favorite place among locals and visitors was a store owned by Mr. Warren called 'H.B. Warren' or 'Casa Warren,' where one could buy most everything that was needed. Faye's fondest memory of the place was sitting on the high stools waiting on her order of the great ham and cheese sandwich, followed by a fabulous vanilla milkshake. No better sandwich or milkshake could be found on the island of Roatan.

There was just one doctor and one dentist in the town. The doctor's name was Dr. Polo Galindo and the dentist's was Dr. Lloyd Cooper. One day, as a young girl, her sister Sadie had taken her to see Dr. Cooper. Just like any other kid would be, she was terrified of even hearing his name mentioned. Just knowing that his needle of Novocaine would soon be pushed into her tender gums was nerve-wracking. Dr. Lloyd Cooper also had a small display of for-sale items on a shelf in his small clinic. Frightful and trembling, the girl was looking at and admiring one item in particular on that shelf: a real gold ring with a blue stone. As a consoling gift to her, her sister bought the gold ring and gave it to her. It was the most beautiful and very first piece of jewelry she ever owned. She would cherish the ring for the rest of her life, for it brought to memory special days with the sister who was like a mother to her and who she dearly loved.

Upon arriving in Coxen Hole safely, the two entered the humble home of Dr. Polo Galindo, which also housed his small and friendly medical clinic. Dr. Polo was an icon among the people of

Roatan, where everyone loved and respected him. He was a fabulous and caring soul who saw to the sick needs of everyone. It mattered not to him if one had money to pay for services at such a time as they were needed, for no one was turned away. Dr. Polo's wife, 'Doñita' as they called her, had the gentlest and sweetest personality of any person that Faye had ever met in her young life. Her sweet accent when she spoke was one that could not soon be forgotten.

Upon seeing the fear in the young girl's eyes, in his caring and gentle way Dr. Polo assured her that everything would be alright. She was then made to lie upon his narrow table while her brother-in-law watched the surgical proceedings. With the big needle that Dr. Polo was holding in his hand spouting its fluid into the air, the doctor started to walk towards her. Faye was ready to run out the door, but it was far more important to have the painful piece of wood removed than to run.

After the surgery, some stitches were required to mend the wound. With a well-bandaged abdomen and a bag of medicine in her hand, she was once again on the back of the dreaded motorcycle, headed back on the curvy Three S's Road to French Harbour.

Note: The goodness within each individual far exceeds what the eye may see or the ear may hear, for if one has goodness within, then it matters not what the tongue may say, for the goodness within is greater than the tongue without.

Section 22

FIRST JOB

With a well-healed abdomen and a tiny scar as a reminder, Faye - now a fifteen-year-old young woman - was still on the island of Roatan, which she had at last come to call home.

It was here that she would get her first real job. This was not a job of Cinderella or Pocahontas as in her younger life, but a job that would give her a sense of accomplishment in the form of a payday. Her job was at the Hyde Fish Factory. Faye and most of her friends all went to work at the same place. The work was challenging - and smelly at that! Working with such seafood was rough on their young, tender hands. But they all reaped paychecks for the first time in their young lives. This money was worth the sacrifice of nicks and pricks to tender hands caused from the handling of fish.

No work was done on Saturday or Sunday. That was their time to spend their hard-earned money and attend church. On Saturday nights, with their money in hand, the girls would make their choices together at the small stores, such as Miss Sibyl's, Mr. Homer's, or Miss Lindy's. Somehow, Faye always found herself at Miss Sybil's store, where she would stand at the counter admiring lovely fabrics of many colors. Those fabrics made lovely dresses, some of which she made herself. She learned this skill early in life from watching her own mother sew. Like her mother, she worked without patterns.

Note: It is shameful for any parent to teach their children nothing, for in so doing they have failed to make a great contribution to society.

Section 23

HER FATHER'S VISITS

Faye noticed that her father would make more and more visits by dory from Barbarat to Roatan. He would stay for a day or two at her sister's house. This would occur at the times when her mother was there. They never knew when he would show up, but they became accustomed to the engine sounds made by his dory. They would hear that particular dory engine coming down the canal which ran directly in front of her sister's house, and they knew then that it was him. Faye's mother would immediately get sick from anger and grief. The young woman suffered such moments of fear on behalf of her mother's frightful condition that at times she would frantically run to seek medical attention that could help her mother. After a time, her parents would be seen talking from time to time.

By this time, the would-be boyfriends on French Harbour were plentiful for the choosing. But none would be found who could steal her young, innocent heart as of yet. At one time, a certain boat came from Utila to Roatan to pick up cargo. On this boat also came a young man who Faye had known all her life. Over the years, she would see him here and there during her brief visits home to Utila. The young man found out where her sister's house was and came looking for her. That day, he declared his love for her and tried to give her his ring. The girl politely rejected the offer, for he could not steal her young, innocent heart. At this point, she found no suitor and was not looking for one.

Note: When anger is allowed to live, it will destroy its dwelling place, for anger is a tool that one must learn to bury while it is yet alive.

Section 24

RETURN TO UTILA

The day had finally come when Faye's sister Sadie needed to have a talk with her. The sad look that was upon her sister's face was unrecognizable to the young woman. It would appear that her sister had tears forming in her eyes. The sixteen-year-old was given what should have been the best news that anyone could have giver her - news that she waited on for years. Henry had made a decision to open a store of his own and would no longer be gone to sea. She was no longer needed to live in Roatan, but was welcome to stay if she so desired.

The news was so unexpected that the young woman didn't immediately know what to say. By now, her sister and brother-in-law had become like parents to her and she loved them the same way that she knew they loved her. The two had given her a very good life in spite of her earlier unsettlement to Roatan. By now she had long been attached to her Jackson family and especially to her young nephews, Andall and Dale. The boys were attached to her as well, for she could seldom go anywhere without the two wanting to follow.

Tears formed in the girl's eyes as she thought about the time when her sister was doing the ironing and little Andall uttered one of his first sentences as he said "Mama iron daddy clothes." She also thought of the time little Dale went missing while everyone frantically searched for him until he was finally found along the lagoon's edge, sailing a little boat that he had constructed all by himself. On and on, beautiful memories of the two little nephews ran through her young mind - memories so real that they caused her to carry a heavy heart where the boys were concerned. Even though she was just a young woman, she felt as though these two were her very own.

But what surprised her most was that she had also learned to love this great island of Roatan and to leave it was to cast another void in her young life. By now, some changes had already been on the uphill climb, as new constructions were happening all over the island in preparation for bigger things to come. Airplanes now landing on the newly formed airport in Coxen Hole were plentiful, as tourism was now getting its big foot into Roatan's door. The Three S's Highway was no longer a slippery, red clay road, but was now a nice, paved road that was busy with taxis running up and down its curvy turns, transporting passengers to and from Coxen Hole, French Harbour, and the other settlements further east and west.

For Faye, the news was too much too soon and she needed a few days to think about these new developments that would once again bring changes to her life. No longer the little barefoot girl, she was now a fully-grown young woman of sixteen. Her young mind was greatly troubled as it played back scenes of Zero candy bars, Coca-Colas, swimming races, and all the other wonderful things she had encountered on the island. Taking refuge in her place of isolation for some hours, she watched as the pigeons, from their limbs in the trees, fluttered their wings in preparation for new flights that would take them to new destinations.

With her decision made, she headed back home to her sister to give her the news. She would be returning back home to Utila. But her eyes would not yet see the dramatic change that awaited her on Utila. Once her decision was made, a new joy was mounting within the young woman. The joy was akin to what one would experience upon finding a treasured piece of something that was lost for a long time. One could not so easily forget the land that they love, rich with childhood memories of play places and days gone by. It was in these places, as a child, that she often played childhood games, reminisced while visiting her popular fishing spot or the trees that she climbed, and hunted pigeons.

Faye now packed not the girlish cotton dresses, but a new kind of clothing, gently folding them and placing them into her new suitcase. The old bee was leaving Roatan, the second home that she had come to love. Days later, she would board a small plane headed back to Utila. During these years, Utila had acquired a small, rocky, dirt airstrip located on the very point of the island's ocean edge.

She hurriedly looked up old playmates who had also turned into nice-looking young women and who were a joy with which to reunite. Her mother, still doing the same hard work of baking coconut bread and sewing clothes, was happy to have her long-gone daughter home again. Faye quickly took up the slack to help out as she always had in her younger life.

It was not long before would-be boyfriends started hanging around or sending messages by friends to make their interest in her known, but the young woman was content with having them as group friends. After the nightly walks around town, they would all hang out on her front porch for silly laughs and conversation. Slaps were still being administered as they continued to try and hold her hand or steal a kiss.

As time went on, she continued to visit back and forth to Roatan, where friends and family awaited her and where she would still hide from such would-be boyfriends!

Note: The tender innocence that any young person is fortunate to find must be guarded to the fullest, for when innocence is gone it can never be replaced.

Section 25

ALMOST HOMELESS

The sixteen-year-old Faye was having some difficulty adjusting to her new life on Utila, for she had returned to encounter a greater change to her way of life. Had she been the same little girl as in times past, then to her it would have mattered not. To the child dreamer, such a thing as this would never have dampened her spirit in the least. Now, the young woman that she was could only wish that she could go back to dreaming about pirates and treasure. This great change which she was now experiencing was the fault of the same hurricane, Francelia, which had found the people of Roatan when she was changed from a girl to a woman.

As was customary to the island men, once they had fair warning of Francelia - which came by radio - they would go from house to house, warning the people to vacate their homes and head to higher ground for safety. Families could be seen with pillowcases of necessary items and their little ones in tow, swiftly walking through the streets as they sought safety. A common place of safety to the people was upon the hill. The people who lived upon the higher grounds called 'the hill' would open their homes to anyone and everyone who required a place of safety. It would sometimes be days until it was safe for families to return back to their homes. This type of hospitality from her neighbors made Faye proud to call herself an islander.

That day was a sad one for her family. As Faye waded through the ankle-deep water in her delicate, womanly condition while the family took shelter in the home of Mrs. Minnie Jackson, she was unaware of what was happening with her family in Utila as they also took shelter. On that day, the claws of the monster hurricane, with its clutches opened wide, laid hold upon their simple but homey wooden house, lifting it from the posts on which it stood and dropping it lop-sided in the island sand. The young woman was having trouble adjusting to her new living conditions.

By this time she had quite a few admirers, as she was now a nice-looking young lady. She was of average height and weight and easily identified by a lovely, shapely teenage figure. She had a fair complexion with a few small freckles on her nose and cheeks. Her eyes were coffee brown in color and her reddish-brown hair hung midway down her back.

Faye at 16 years of age

Like any other normal sixteen-year-old young lady would be, she was embarrassed of her living conditions. However, her lop-sided house never stopped the admirers from seeking her company or congregating on her front porch. In fact, nothing had changed where friends were concerned. There were some who desired the status of boyfriend without any luck, for the young lady was of the belief that her heart would talk to her when the time was right for such things as a boyfriend. A couple of the would-be boyfriends who would try to lend comfort to her in regards to her embarrassment of her home told her that they came to see what was in the house and not the house itself! She figured that that was a smart move on their part, but it still earned them no points. Little by little she would begin to adjust to her surroundings.

Note: When one cannot change one's environment, one has nothing else to do but to accept and live, for happiness should never be measured by the abundance of what one has, but by the peace that comes from within.

Section 26

THE HUNT

Still in the same lop-sided house, with the young woman's mother now working full time and her sister Muriel also working, Faye was left with a lot of responsibility at home. For one so young to have such responsibilities of daily existence, she used them to her advantage as lessons well-learned.

As a sixteen-year-old young woman and settled again at home in Utila, life for Faye would continue, bringing with it memories of past trauma. The young woman finally made peace within herself and decided that one can't control any of the unfortunate, horrid incidents that sometimes come our way - especially when such incidents happen through no fault of one's own. In the case of unavoidable circumstances, one has no choice but to learn to somehow live again.

As she had done so many times in her younger life, the young woman would gather together a machete and fishing line and make her way in that same little wooden canoe in search of a favorite fishing spot, numb to such danger as could be awaiting her again. She would paddle through the dark water lagoon that, once away from the main body of water, wound its way through much narrower passageways. With mangroves heavily lining both sides of the lagoon, her canoe continued to areas of complete isolation.

She never considered the decision not to go, for had she not gone perhaps there would have been no fish that would do well when added to the meager meal of red beans and rice. This made a tasty meal and it was customary for the islanders to prepare such a meal as red beans and rice on a daily basis. There was no child that complained of such meager meals, for they were taught that a belly full was a belly full regardless, as should be taught still - for today we raise a generation of wastefulness.

On many other occasions the young woman, along with a group of friends, would make their way on foot or by canoe after darkness had fallen to the more desolate or swampy areas of the island in search of the island's famous blue land crab. Over the centuries, this had fed many hungry families. These crabs could be found by the hundreds as they scurried about the ground in search of food or even a mate. The crustaceans had very large pinchers that, if one was not educated in how to catch them, could inflict a mighty painful pincer bite... or worse. The common custom was to grab them barehanded by their backs and toss them into a crocus sack held open by a partner. These were large, fast-moving crabs that lived in deep holes in the ground, so one had to be swift in the technique of crab catching. Needless to say, Faye became a very good crab catcher from an early age.

Once the friends had a sack or two of crabs they would make their way back home to prepare for the crab boiling event. The crabs would be boiled along with green bananas still in their peels. They were then enjoyed along with onions steeped in fresh lime juice or cider vinegar, salt, and black pepper, which were prepared before the hunt ever began. This was a tradition and a favorite but messy late-night meal to islanders of all ages.

Many days would also find the young woman with a sack in hand as she waded in waist-deep salt water in search of conch. Conch was plentiful to families, but it was not so easy to obtain this seafood that was common to the island.

Note: Responsibilities and lessons well-learned should be applied to one's life, for should the need arise for such skills, one is - without question - equipped to survive for it's amazing what one can learn to do when one has no choice but to learn. We should become a people who are willing to learn new things to our betterment and enjoyment of life.

Section 27

THE SERENADE

A sixteen-year-old young woman and her house were still sitting lop-sided in the sand and she was even more shameful of it. Yet she had a host of would-be boyfriends still hanging around in the evenings. But the lop-sided house sitting upon the ground was an easy escape for the young woman. There were times when older single - or even divorced - gentlemen would come to the house to sit in the swing and have conversation with her. But the young woman was no fool. Upon hearing their voices drifting from the porch to her bedroom, she would easily make her escape through the already-opened window and make her way to friends' homes, or even to town, without ever being seen. Those gentlemen would then be left on the porch with just her mother for conversation! The young woman did this time and time again.

It was common for the young men that had a crush on a girl to serenade her with music. Sometimes there would be a group of them that would go from house to house with their music. The girls would be awakened late into the night by the sound of music playing in the street or their yards. It was an exciting time of wonderment regarding who was doing the serenading and who it was that had a crush on the young lady within. The girls would never find out - at least not during the serenade - because mothers would not allow their girls to open a window to see!

Life was getting good again on Utila Island.

Note: Society should again long for such simplicity of innocence brought to past generations of children who relished in the fun-filled simple things of life.

Section 28

FIRST KISS

The sixteen-year-old young lady was a strange one. It mattered not to her that, at her age, kissing boys was the popular thing to do. Her ideas about kissing were her own and she always figured that since her heart was not yet stolen, her kisses would remain her very own. She would stick to her own beliefs that such a private and memorable occasion as a first kiss was one to be waited on and treasured, and that the one who was special enough to receive her kiss should be counted worthy. A kiss is like a word spoken - once it is given it can never be taken back. And especially if the young man in question was undeserving of such an important give-away as a kiss.

The young lady attended many birthday parties with friends who relished in the famous kissing game called 'spin the bottle.' She somehow would avoid being kissed by any of the young men who were popular for kissing. Such young men were the talk among many of the young ladies. Many times, the young men would try their proficient kisses on her without any luck. To her, it was her way and her decision who she would allow to have that very special first kiss.

Note: When any human would preserve such personal beliefs as to one's desires, it should be counted as a great achievement to one's life.

Section 29

TRICKED

Her cousin who she dearly loves, Wilson Howell, tricked her. The two were as close as any decent cousinly relationship could get. They were singing partners who enjoyed each other's company with their silly humor and laughs. Both had a special singing gift within them. On many occasions the two would either sit in Aunt Joy's swing on the front porch or in Faye's swing. Wilson would play his guitar and the singing would begin.

Faye's cousin, Wilson Howell.

Somehow, they always managed to gather a listening audience in the street. The two would, for hours, sing the popular love songs of the time, such as "Walk Through this World with Me," "Dark Moon," "Help Me Make It Through the Night," "He'll Have to Go," and "Welcome to My World." On and on they would sing, at times even walking through the streets of Utila singing and playing the guitar. On Sunday evenings they would visit the elderly in their homes and sing to them.

These times hold such great memories for Faye that she would not change them even if she could.

Utila Commandant Building, Main Street.

This same loved cousin Wilson, upon finding out that she had never been kissed, quickly ran - without her knowledge - to disclose such personal information to a favorite young man of good character that he figured would be a suitable first. This was a very good-looking young man that she had known her entire life. Wilson told the young man that she wanted him to be the one to which she would give her first kiss. He also told him that she would wait for him while taking her walk with friends that night. But the young woman had not said any such thing to her cousin! The young man found her that night, and she can still see the grin on his face - the reason for which only he knew.

As to the rest of the kissing matter, the young woman leaves it to the wonderment of your imaginative minds as to whether or not she let the young man have that very special first kiss, and who the young man could have been. She knows that many of you who know her will short-circuit your brains trying to figure out just who that young man was! Or perhaps that same young man, should he get his hands on this book, will enjoy a prideful moment

and spill the beans! Ah, those wonderful teenage years! Who can forget them?

Note: Ties of closeness as to a friend or relative should forever be anchored in the mind for safekeeping where no wind or wave of

heresies can destroy it.

Section 30

TAKEN AWAY TO BARBARAT ISLAND AGAIN

Barbarat Island

Faye, now seventeen years old, had finally allowed her young heart to be stolen by a decent, wonderful, and caring young man who was respectful of her personal notions about such things as courtship. His respect towards her was a quality that she greatly admired, for few would possess these admirable qualities. The young woman had finally found her young love.

Faye and her family would continue to make visits to Roatan Island, where she would again reunite with family and old friends.

Again, without warning, a storm would surround her life. Her mother had decided to give her husband another chance with his family. Faye was to have another chance to live with the father that she grew up without and one with which she shared no bond.

But at the same time, the young woman still possessed a love for him as a daughter should to the father who gave her life.

By giving him another chance with his family, the young woman would now be uprooted once again and forced to leave her new-found, happy life behind as they returned back to Barbarat, the island still uninhabited by humans. At this time, Faye's Uncle Dickie and his family had already left Barbarat. Now the torture would be even more unbearable. The young woman's life was turning into a terrible, disastrous nightmare filled with pain and anguish that only she knew awaited her.

Saying her goodbyes to special friends was not easy, especially when she tried to hide her emotional state of mind. During the hours-long dory ride in rough seas and hot sun, the young woman was quietly beside herself. She had always been a silent sufferer, even through the traumatic experience of years ago.

As her father's dory approached the island of Barbarat and her eyes fell upon the little wooden house that would become her prison, she could not stop the flow of tears that escaped her young brown eyes. With a torment so deep that perhaps only she could understand, she sat in the dory trying to hide the tears that were now flowing down her face like a waterfall. What teenager, she wondered, could be happy in such a place as this island of isolation? And what teenager could be happy being separated from a new-found happiness?

Upon making land at the small dock that she well remembered from long ago, her small feet became as lightning rods of speed as her sandals flew from her feet, sending grains of beach sand trailing behind as she fled from the only living beings on the island of Barbarat. As though she were in her former little girl's body and with a familiar speed, the young woman ran - giving freedom to emotions that no longer needed to be contained. Running up the beach without giving thought to the small, sharp rocks making contact with her tender feet, she fled in desperate need of solitude. Flopping down in the white beach sand and burying her head in her knees, the dam holding back the flow broke loose as rivers of tears cascaded down her face.

Hours passed as she stared out to the endless sea of nothingness with no view of an iron shore as waves foamed and crashed against its blackness, longing and mourning for her home. Deep in her thoughts of grief as self-pity overtook her, she wondered how so many things could have befallen her in her young life. The questions she asked within herself were many. What did she do wrong to cause such chaos to her young self? First, as a child brought to this very island, she was forced to leave behind playful friends and games in the street. She was then left behind on Roatan. And then there was the horrid incident of years ago and the return to Utila and now, once again, back to Barbarat. Who knew if this would even be the end of such chaos? How many times could she endure being uprooted from the home with which she was in love? With these thoughts came a fresh batch of tears.

Weeks turned into months; walking the deserted beaches of Barbarat and sitting in the turquoise water eating sea grapes and cocoplums day after day soon got old. Limbs of the ripe grapes that hung by the clusters as they touched the ocean's surface were an inherently beautiful sight, but they held no beauty to the unhappy young woman.

Playing love songs on the record player made her cry. She would listen to such songs and burst into a new flood of tears, especially upon hearing the one called "Help Me Make It Through the Night." Those love songs added to the pain she was experiencing in full force.

The young woman was happier when it came time for the midday meal, for her father had employed a few locals from Helene to help with the coconut harvesting. Her mother, with her help, would prepare the meal and serve it to the crew while they sat at the wooden table on the back porch.

Among the crew was a Mr. Victor James of Helene. Mr. Victor had become a friend to the family and it was Faye's pleasure to serve him. Since he was one of her favorites, she always tried to see to it that he had a little extra added to his plate. When Faye would make pineapple tarts from the pineapples that grew in the yard, she always saved one or two for Mr. Victor. He would reward her with her favorite sweet, coconut sponge, or a straw hat full of pink, fluffy cocoplums.

There were two things that kept her sane through this transition of her unhappy life.

One was the love letters that she received on a daily basis from her young love at home. All mail was delivered by dory to the island of Helene, which was about an hour dory ride from Barbarat. The girl's father would bring the letters in the late evening upon his return to Barbarat from Helene, for he would continue to be involved with his other families who lived in the settlement. Her father would get angry about the letters and complained that her boyfriend needed to get his own post office!

The second was that on Saturdays her father would take them on the hour-long dory ride to Helene, where Faye and her mother and sister would spend the night at the home of Mrs. Eunela Bowman in preparation for Sunday service. Mrs. Bowman was a wonderful and friendly lady who was a good friend to Faye's mother, along with Mazie and Gloria Bodden and Jocelyn James. The young woman looked forward to such church services, which her mother and sister also attended, where she would find temporary peace from her troubled heart.

With everyone in Helene knowing that the young woman had a nice singing voice, she was always asked to sing to the people. And sing she did, for when she sang her heart was made lighter and her sorrows would temporarily disappear. Singing always made her forget her pain, disappointments, and anger.

It was there on Helene that she would become good friends with two young ladies, Orlena and Cheryl. At times, these two young ladies would pass a few days with Faye and her sister Muriel on Barbarat. These visits among friends were like a small piece of heaven to the young woman's sanity.

An escape from her prison of isolation that could have been possible, but one which she never considered, was a pilot who came to Barbarat from the mainland bringing supplies to the surrounding areas. Faye would watch from the edge of the dirt airstrip as the small plane landed. At times, she was the only one at the isolated air strip. The pilot tried his advances upon the young woman, but she would escape his grip. He would later find her in Utila and continue his advances many times after. This would continue for months without success.

A few years later, she was saddened to learn of his death, as he was killed in a plane crash.

Note: When one remains true to one's self, it is because a great knowledge resides within which can never be compromised.

Section 31

HOME AT LAST

Faye (right) and sister, Muriel on Utila bridge.

In the end, Faye's mother and father's relationship did not work out. It was now time for her and the family to head back to life on civilized Utila. A happiness that the young woman had once experienced was renewed. She was happy yet shy to see her young love again. The young man had waited for her return home. Life was better and she felt alive again.

After some time had passed, her young life again changed unexpectedly. An unusual opportunity presented itself to the young woman. She was asked by American missionaries who had met her in church during a series of services to accompany them for a visit to the United States. The visit would last for a few months before she would return home. It was not an easy decision for the young lady or her mother to make, so her Grandmother Tae Tae would make the decision for them. The decision was made. She was to go with the missionaries. She would soon find herself making preparations to leave her island home yet again, but with all intentions of returning to Utila.

Faye Whitefield age 18.

Note: We never know where life will eventually lead us, but we must all be willing to lead or be led by a higher power.

Section 32

GRAND FINALE OF THE STORY:

THE WEDDING

AND THE AUTHOR

The little barefoot girl who climbed almond trees and chased iguanas **is the very author of this book: Faye Whitefield Carlton of Utila Bay Island.**

During the preparations for the visit to the United States, I was now just past eighteen years of age. Shortly after my arrival to the new country, I met a young minister who asked me very quickly to become his bride. My first reply to him was "I did not come to your country seeking a husband!" My answer was no. The young man was very insistent that I marry him! He again asked me to become his bride while in the United States. Again my answer was no. The marriage proposals would continue over the next couple of months.

After a time, I gave in and said yes. But my yes was conditional in two ways. First, he had to write a letter of proposal to my mother asking for my hand in marriage, for this was the way that it was done on my island home. Second, my yes was based upon my wedding taking place on my island home of Utila. If he couldn't handle either of the two, that would be the end of it.

Soon after the engagement, I made preparations to return back home to Utila. My visit had now turned into seven months. I was now well past eighteen years old and still the innocent young woman that I had always been.

Upon my return home with news of my impending nuptials, my mother did not freak out. She always knew of my track record where my thinking was concerned. She had also received the letter from the young man asking for my hand in marriage. The plan was that my expected husband would follow me to Utila in three weeks' time. However, my mother was very clear that not one pound of flour for a wedding cake would be bought until he had set his feet on 'the rock,' meaning Utila!

On the day that I knew he was to arrive, I headed to the gravel airstrip to await the small plane that would bring him the eighteen miles from the mainland to Utila. Of course, my sister Muriel and cousin Delany both chased me to see for themselves if he would actually show up! I was a bundle of nerves, for the two of them were working me over.

As was customary for the islanders, both young and old were at the airstrip waiting to see who was returning home from the United States. People were everywhere. Many eager eyes watched the distant skies for the approach of the airplane. Once the plane was spotted, cries of excitement could be heard from everyone. The airplane landed and the few passengers, one by one, got out of the plane.

My expected was nowhere to be seen. The landing of the airplane was within yards of the onlookers. Even though I had faith in my expected, my discouragement came at the expense of my sister Muriel and my cousin Delany mocking me! The onlookers stared, open-mouthed, for everyone on the island knew of my approaching wedding.

"That's what you get," screamed my sister Muriel, "for marrying a gringo!" Gringo meant 'dirty foreigner' or Yankee.

Another plane was scheduled for the following day, but my pride would not allow me to go back to that airstrip! I continued to be persecuted by my sister concerning the gringo. My mother had nothing to say.

Old Utila Airport on the point. Fotee standing on the right.

The next morning, the *Bonnie J* from Roatan, captained by my brother-in-law Henry, made it to Utila with my sister Sadie and the boys, Andall and Dale. Family, friends, bridesmaids, some of my adopted Jackson family, and many others were all ready and excited for my wedding, which was to take place at 4 pm. But a wedding was impossible without a groom. My father also made his appearance to attend my wedding, but - for reasons which I never knew - he refused to walk me down the aisle.

The wedding guests, along with some locals, waited on the porch of my still lop-sided house with looks of wonder and whispers of questions, as they were in awe of the events. The locals who had gathered in the street and in my yard were obviously gossiping about the wedding stand-up. By now, news had spread all over the island of the 'gringo wedding stander-upper.' Whispers of "Poor Faye; it's just unheard of what's happened to her" could be heard among the locals. Some also whispered about what a shameful tragedy it would be if I were with child.

The next plane was due to arrive at 2 pm. I was still determined to not return to the airstrip to suffer more ridicule. By around 2:15 I was locked away in my bedroom when I heard excited voices outside. I made my way to the front door to see what the commotion was about. Getting out of Fotee's old, beat-up, rusty truck was my expected! The crowd was gathered around him as they looked him over. Our neighbor, Mrs. Ena Cooper, yelled from across her yard "Jesus has come!"

My expected immediately gave an explanation for his tardiness: passport services in Miami had delayed his passport by one day.

At that time, telephone service was not yet available in Utila. I then asked him how he knew where to find me, since I was not at the airstrip to meet him. He said that as soon as he stepped from the airplane Fotee said to him "Get in the truck." When he asked why, Fotee said to him "Do you want to go to Faye or not?" What he didn't know was that when Fotee saw him, he figured that he had to be the 'wedding stander-upper gringo,' for strangers to the island were few.

My love and faith in him accepted his explanation and preparations for the wedding were immediately underway. He would arrive to the same lop-sided house that was home to me. My family had just that day to meet him before we would be wed the next.

On the day of his arrival, preparations of wedding cakes and the likes were underway in full force. Family, friends, guests, and neighbors all helped to prepare for the event. This wedding was big news to our small island, especially because of the 'stander-upper gringo.'

As was customary to the island, everyone was invited, for wedding announcements were posted on a chalk board in the town square with the knowledge that practically the whole island would show up. It hardly needed announcing, for anything and everything that was happening on Utila was always known by everyone and remains so till this day. Such is the custom of my island people that I dearly love, for we are all blood of one blood.

The wedding took place in my home church, Utila Church of God, with twelve bridesmaids and groomsmen, four flower girls, and a ring bearer. Bridesmaids included childhood friends from Roatan. My sister Muriel refused to be my maid-of-honor, for she was always a shy one. My cousin Delany took her place. The singing partner, Wilson Howell, served as best man to my expected. Signed witnesses to the matrimony were Talbert Cooper and Leland Howell. Since my father refused to walk me down the aisle - for reasons of which I did not ask - his brother, Reverend Hoover Whitefield, took his place. The ceremony was officiated by Rev. Fred Cooper, pastor of the Utila Methodist Church.

My family starting from the left: Muriel, my mother (Nonie), my husband (Chuck), Faye, my dad (Morley), Sadie, Andall, and Dale Jackson

Two weeks later, I would again leave my island home of Utila to begin a new life as a new bride in the United States.

A couple of years later, I would make a return visit back to Utila only to find that the lop-sided house was gone! My brother Gilbert and brother-in-law Henry had built a brand new one for my mother!

My friend Cheryl Diaz of Helene went on to become pastor of the Helene Church of God, where she still serves to this day.

As for my friend Orlena Bodden, also of Helene, I know not of her whereabouts, but would love to see her again someday.

My cousin, Wilson Howell of Utila, went on to become pastor of the Utila Church of God, where he remains to this day.

My nephews Andall and Dale Jackson went on to become the owners of successful businesses on Roatan that are still in operation today. Dale also went on to serve as the elected mayor of Roatan.

After my move to the United States, it would be ten months and twenty-one days until I would become a mother to a beautiful baby girl. I fell in love all over again. That marriage would bring me another daughter and a son who, like his father, became a pastor at an early age. The daughters, like their mother, became gifted gospel singers. Between the three, I have been blessed with six lovely grandchildren! And the stander-upper gringo remains a minister to this day.

And the young lady, Faye Whitefield, who forty-one years ago said "I do" to the young stander-upper gringo, Charles Carlton, remains married to him to this day!

The girl from the Bay Islands is still singing and is always with happy expectations of her next visit home to Utila and Roatan, the Bay Islands of Honduras - where sweet friends, amazing sunsets, and out-of-this-world diving, snorkeling, and much more await my return to the islands that I still call home!

Note: It matters not if the places in which we have lived can be counted as sheep scattered upon a hillside; we cannot and should not ever settle to forget the lands that we called home!

The End

HISTORY OF THE BAY ISLANDS

Christopher Columbus would discover for himself, the Bay Islands as he made landfall at Guanaja Island on the morning of July 30th, 1502, during his fourth voyage to the New World, a discovery which would change the world of today's islanders. Sighting a high island covered with pines, Mr. Columbus would set his feet upon Soldado Beach on the north side of the island. He claimed it, of course, for Spain.

Notably, this was the first time that the admiral would come across cacao, which is the core of chocolate.

The Bay Islands' rich cultural diversity stems from the variety of people that have inhabited them over the many ages. Today's inhabitants are the descendants of natives, Africans, and Europeans, including pirates and mainland Hondurans. The islands' original inhabitants were Paya Indians. The Paya were a nomadic group of hunter-gatherers and fishermen who traveled in canoes between the islands and the mainland to trade goods among themselves and with the Mayans and other tribes from the mainland.

Over the following centuries, the island of Roatan would be caught between Spanish and British rule. During these years, pirates numbering over 5,000 invaded the island of Roatan, but in 1650 the Spaniards were able to drive the pirates out. At this time, most of the island's original inhabitants were forced into slavery or relocated. It wasn't until 1797, when English soldiers relocated 3,000 black Carib-African Indians from St. Vincent to

Roatan, that the Bay Islands received their first permanent settlers. These people are now known as the Garifuna, and while most of the original Garifuna resettled in Trujillo on the mainland, Roatan's town of Punta Gorda has remained the first town of the Garifuna.

In 1830, immigrants from the Cayman Islands first arrived in Utila and eventually spread to the other Bay Islands. The islanders today predominantly speak a unique heavy-accent version of Caribbean English.

While the British reclaimed the Islands in 1852, a short time later they were forced to turn them over to the newly formed Republic of Honduras. At a convention held in Guatemala on April 30, 1859, England - under a great deal of pressure from the United States - agreed to surrender the Bay Islands to the Republic of Honduras, to which the Bay Islands now belong and ever shall belong.

Such is just a small piece of the rich history of our Bay Islands of Honduras: Utila, Roatan, and Guanaja; those islands which I, the girl, am proud to call home.

These islands today hold a spot in world travel and tourism and are frequented by vacationers from around the world who are seeking the perfect getaway via ocean cruise liners or by air, both of which are readily available as access to the Bay Islands. These Bay Islands of Honduras should become of great interest to you as you seek your next perfect getaway. For certain, you will not be disappointed.

This was the island of firsts that the little girl, Faye, called home, for it was the island of Utila, hundreds of years earlier, where her English ancestors had settled.

Note: May it always be as the saying goes that "home is where the heart is," for if such is true, the heart can always be at home regardless of its current location.

Utila, Honduras – A worldwide Top 10 Dive Site

Utila, the best kept secret in the Caribbean and it sits on the largest Mesoamerican barrier reef in the western hemisphere where dazzling arrays of different types of coral form this underwater wilderness, and provide homes and food to hundreds of fish species, marine turtles and sharks.

Along the shore, mangroves provide habitat for fish and shorebirds as well as protect coastal areas from damage associated with hurricanes and strong storms .

 Everything on this little island is in walking distance and where you get the most for your buck!

Hotels, apartments and food are the most reasonable you will find anywhere in the Bay Islands.

The scenery alone is worth the trip to Utila, but the Bay Island is not just a beautiful paradise, it's one of the best places to find a connection to the underwater world.

According to a leading travel guide, **Utila is one of the top 10 dive sites in the world**.

Diving in Utila is ideal, offering warm weather year round and a front row seat to many different species of marine life including snorkeling with whale sharks and where you can obtain your diving certification in just a few days at an almost-No cost price from various dive centers located throughout the island.

For a once in a lifetime diving experience make your reservation with any of the following. **Underwater Vision: www.utilascubadiving.com, Alton's dive center: www.diveinutila.com, or Paradise Divers: www.** Paradisediversutila.com. **Make it today!**

And don't forget to visit **Chepes Beach:** A place to tan your fan in the sand!

While you're browsing through Utila's main street, you should drop in to **Bundu Cafe**, where you will experience good food and a front row seat to everything!

NEPTUNE'S

A UTILA FAVORITE

Neptune's Restaurant at Coral Beach Village, Is a ten-minute boat ride on the '**Blue Bayou** as you go down a canal and through mangroves to the southern shore of Utila.

The perfect 'get away' where you will experience a day of relaxation as you dine from a fabulously prepared menu of fresh fish and other seafood, salads, fresh local fruits and much more.

 Where your dining experience can be indoors while enjoying a full ocean view or just lazing on its white sandy beach with an added benefit of snorkeling, it's awesome coral reef, where you are bound to see a world of sea life including shrimp and lobster.

One thing is certain about Utila, you will be back!

ABOUT ROATAN TODAY

Roatan is the largest of the Bay Islands and is known around the world for its scuba diving enjoyment of the largest Mesoamerican reef in the western hemisphere.

It's no wonder that Roatan now stands as number three in the ten most places to visit in the world! And has become increasingly popular as a stopover for cruise ships where tourists flock to sidewalk markets of colorful island and cultural items.

Roatan has quickly become a world renown vacation favorite as it offers five star resorts with any and everything that one would look for in a tropical vacation.

The pristine white sandy beaches, colorful coral reefs and lush tropical foliage have made this island a paradise. But there is much more to Roatan than its pristine, turquoise waters and world famous dive sites.

It offers a host of island attractions from glass bottom boats, to jungle parks, private tours and much more that's suitable for all ages who are out for a carefree and fun filled family vacation.

Roatan's beaches are some of the best in the Caribbean. The reef protected waters are ideal for snorkeling, kayaking, swimming with dolphins and a myriad of other water activities such as snorkeling at the Bay Islands underwater museum where you will see a lost Mayan civilization of artifacts as they lay on the oceans floor.

Plan your next vacation to Roatan, Honduras.

For your tour pleasure contact, jjacksontour@yahoo.com or call 011-504-3321-7942.

A FAMILY FAVORITE

Reviews taken from satisfied customers:

My friends and I had such a great time here!!!It is an amazing location. So many fish and sea creatures everywhere.

An underwater museum loaded with history as conveyed by native islanders. Dip back in time and experience the rich history of the Mayan world under water.

As you swim through history on their snorkel tour, you see lots of aquatic life, while submerging yourself in coral filled alluring beauty. This was by far one of my favorite things to do..

For a fun filled day with the family, a visit to this under sea museum should be on your list of to do's!   For contact information: www.underwatermuseumroatan.com

Frank Morgan

A Utila Mogul

FRANK MORGAN, a man who wasn't afraid of hard work, a man who was responsible for bringing various ' firsts' to Utila.

Mr. Morgan, some decades ago, brought some excitement to the people of Utila, when he brought the first vehicle to the island . And it's engine can still be seen laying around keeping company with its surrounding metal buddies in the town's vicinity.

To name a couple of his accomplishments, is my great honor to do so as he did much for the betterment of Utila island.

Mr. Morgan, for many years, served as agent for SAHSA Airlines during its early maiden voyages to Utila, where it first landed on the gravel airstrip on the South side of Utila's point.

He was also responsible for establishing the islands first ice factory where 100 pound blocks of ice was cut to size, to meet the people's needs.

Such squares of ice that was sold for as little as five cents was a welcome to the island people!

Thank you, Mr. Morgan, for your contribution to the people of Utila island.

DR. POLO GALINDO

A LOCAL HERO OF ROATAN

Dr. Policarpo Galindo Ebanks was born in West End, Roatan on Dec 25, 1910. When he was 18 years old, Galindo was hired by a hospital in Castilla as a general assistant. For the next 13 years, Galindo worked through all the Honduras departments in the hospitals, learning about surgery, dentistry and obstetrics.

In 1941, Galindo married Doña Margarita Sosa and they moved back to Roatan.

Many Islanders knew of Galindo's medical experience and came to visit him and ask for advice.

In the next several years, Galindo opened a clinic and drugstore in Coxen Hole and was treating a high volume of patients for various ailments. Even though he never attended medical school and lacked any formal education, Polo Galindo became known to Islanders as Dr. Polo.

Dr. Galindo traveled by horseback and dory to make house calls at all hours of the day or night, delivering many children across the island. In the late 1950s, several people attempted to stop Dr. Galindo from practicing medicine due to his informal education.

Islanders demonstrated against this action, protesting on the streets of Coxen Hole with signs showing support for Dr. Polo Galindo.

His hobby was cattle ranching and he found great joy in spending time with his wife and their five children. After 51 years of operating his clinic, in 1993, Dr. Galindo treated his last patient.

On February 20, 1995, Dr. Polo Galindo, died at the age of 85.

After his death, a medical clinic in Punta Gorda was named in his honor.

Dr. Polo Galindo, was loved by the people of Roatan, and his departure from this life left a void in the hearts and lives of many.

ALBERT JACKSON

A ROATAN BUSINESS ICON

Albert Jackson, a man with a vision and heart for the people of Roatan was among some of the very first businessmen to jump start the island of Roatan as we know it today.

His good heart for the betterment of his island people goes without saying as he helped thousands of needy people throughout his lifetime.

Mr. Jackson was responsible for establishing the first Texaco Oil Distribution Center in French Harbour Roatan, where he transported fuel throughout the Bay Islands.

A few of his early business accomplishments were two cargo boats called ' Bonnie J. and Cheryl J, followed by a host of Shrimp Boats.

One of his earliest businesses was 'Jackson Enterprises Hardware & Marine Supply.

He would later form a successful seafood company called ' Blue Water Seafood.'

Within a few short years he would build the beautiful 'Fantasy Island Resort which was among the very first to grace Roatan's lovely beaches.

Mr. Jackson was also responsible for bringing to the island a much needed international shipping company called ' Jackson shipping.

These few named accomplishments is in no way ALL of his successes as a leader in Roatan's community, but they are in fact just the tip of the iceberg!.

Albert Jackson of Roatan Bay Island, Honduras, in 2014, rested from his labors of vision as he made his departure from this life into the next .

To *Albert Jackson* I say a great big **'Thank You** from the people of Roatan and from myself 'The little curly haired 'Old Bee' as you always called me!.

It is my honor to pay tribute to your memory.

IN LOVING MEMORY OF MY MOTHER

Nonie Whitefield; mother of Faye

My mother's story is one of great interest. She was loved and known throughout the Bay Islands and was admired by everyone who knew her. My mother was a short, chubby, very brown-skinned woman of the Mayan tribe. This precious little lady - for a lady she was - never got the chance to know her own family. When she was just a day or two old she was taken from her native people on the mainland of Honduras upon a small cargo boat to the island of Utila, just eighteen miles away, to be raised by strangers who would love and care for her as their own.

I would be told three different accounts relating to the day of her birth.

One such account was that an American known by the last name of Donaldson made his way to the Honduran mainland to work in the banana trade with Standard Fruit Company. This man then fathered a son by a Honduran woman who carried the last name of Morazán. This son would also be given the name of Donaldson. It is said that the American would leave the woman and their small son behind as he relocated to a different area in the country. A couple of years later, Mr. Donaldson would be found by the woman with their young son in tow. The woman was now very pregnant with another child who would become my mother.

The very next day, the woman gave birth to her baby girl. Mr. Donaldson, upon holding this precious baby on the veranda of the hospital to which he took the mother to give birth, made a plan. His heart was captured by the baby girl, who caused him to think about his own small son standing at his side. The plan which the American made included giving the baby his last name. This infant girl was then given the name Patricia Leonora Donaldson and later the nickname of 'Nonie.' Mr. Donaldson, knowing the poverty that awaited the newborn, made a snap decision concerning the betterment of his own small son and the baby girl, whom he already loved. Upon looking at these children, he made a quick decision to change his own lifestyle and become a better individual. He would then offer the baby's mother a few gold coins in exchange for the baby girl.

That same day of the baby's birth, Mr. Donaldson learned of a small cargo boat that was headed to the small island of Utila, to which he had never been. This vessel would change the lives of the man, the baby girl, and his small son, for the three would board that boat as passengers. The baby girl would never look upon the face of her mother again.

Another story told was that the American just took the children and fled.

Others said that the child's mother was killed by a banana transporting train in the outback of her small hometown.

As to which of the three stories is true, I suppose we will never know, for if my mother knew of the accounts of her life as told to her by the American, she never once disclosed such knowledge to us. This man, Donaldson, was the man that she would call 'daddy.' He remained a good father to her and his small son for the rest of his days.

I am thankful that the American, Mr. Donaldson, made it possible for this precious child to become my mother, for I am extremely proud to be called the daughter of Patricia Leonora Donaldson - a great mother to her children.

The truth would not be told if I were to say that I never think upon my ancestral Mayan roots, the people of my mother and myself. For the fact is that, upon my visits to the mainland, I often wondered if this one or that one could be my relatives, for they bore likenesses to my mother.

My mother, 'Nonie,' would grow up to marry a local islander, Hardwick Gilbert Whitefield - better known as Morley - a descendent of early English settlers to the island of Utila.

Had Mr. Donaldson not passed away before my birth, he would be known to me as Granddaddy Donaldson. I regret that I never had the chance to know him, for a grandfather's love I never knew.

Mr. Donaldson married the daughter of the woman, Hester Flynn, who owned the boarding house where the young girl and boy were cared for, as were many other unfortunate children. The woman would hand over her daughter, Dorothy Flynn - better known as 'Tae Tae' - in marriage to Mr. Donaldson. Tae Tae would become a mother to the two children and a grandmother to me.

Flynn house where Faye's mother was raised.

From the time I was a small child, the two of us had many an adventure together! Two favorites come to mind.

One was when we would run all over the island to collect dried almond seeds which were scattered by the hundreds on the ground underneath the large trees on the point. The two of us would pop open the seeds with a hammer, adding the fresh nuts to the pile. Together, we would then make a delicious almond candy!

The second memory is of when this precious grandmother would endlessly drill my young mind with recitals of the lessons she would teach me, such as the 23rd Psalm of the Bible. These lessons were drilled until I was able to fully memorize

From this marriage between Tae Tae and Donaldson came a son who was given the name of Erle Conrad Donaldson, who is still alive and resides in Oklahoma with his family in the United States.

This uncle, who I now call "Tio" when we speak via telephone, was a great, caring brother to my mother.

Left to right: Erle Conrad Donaldson, Dorothy Flynn (Tae Tae), Faye's mother Nonie.

From the Author

I am a true citizen of the

Caribbean. I was born in Utila, Bay Island, Honduras, and grew up in Utila and the surrounding islands of Roatan before finally settling down at age nineteen as a new bride in a strange and foreign country, the United States of America, where I - along with my husband - successfully raised two daughters and one son.

The wide variety of life experience that I gleaned from these Bay Islands in my early years has contributed much inspiration and savvy to the person I am today. The hardships, joys, and challenges that I faced as a young girl taught me not just how to survive, but how to thrive and rise above misfortunes in order to grab life by the tail and run with it! Talk about cultural exposure! I had that and then some! It was these experiences that led me to write my first book, "Daffney's Island Adventures," and this one, "Island Hummingbird."

In addition to being an author, I work hard at being a good wife, mother, grandmother, caregiver, friend, and singer; these are my great contributions to society and life. I spend a great deal of time reading books, learning new songs, listening to love songs that make me cry time and time again, and channeling my ancestral roots through my love for Caribbean and Latin music!

My main goal in this life is to make a difference in the lives of the people with whom I come in contact. To accomplish this, I first strive to be true to God and myself and to possess more kindness in my little finger than most possess in their entire bodies, for kindness is gravely missing in today's society. My second objective is to remain the positive, energetic, aura-filled, loving, funny, and caring woman that I am today! As a writer, I strive to make readers dream big and to cause their hearts to beat a little faster as they reminisce about their own childhood experiences - including the good, the bad, and the ugly. All our experiences are immensely important in molding us into the wonderful, loving, and caring individuals that we are today.

We should always seek the gift of kindness and shower it upon those both near and far. It is my opinion that a successful person is one who finds joy and pleasure in sharing company with friends and strangers alike and who never tears down, but rather builds up, other human beings in the act of kindness.

I flourish with the love of happy expectations for my next visit to the islands I call home, where I reunite with family and friends and excitedly visit those favorite places from my childhood that always held me spellbound!

For contact information, I can be reached via e-mail at fayewhitefieldcarlton@gmail.com, or by phone, (850) 381-9805.